D1373148

ANGEL ON SKIS

Angel on Skis

BETTY CAVANNA

ILLUSTRATED BY ISABEL DAWSON

WILLIAM MORROW AND COMPANY
NEW YORK

To the two Janeys—
who introduced me to Peru, to Christie,
and to the Bromley slopes.

Fourteen

CHAPTER   *one*

THE SCUFFED AND WORN SKIS—one with a split tip—
leaned against the clapboard siding of the farmhouse porch, inviting Angela to come outside.

She looked at the kitchen floor, tracked and
muddy, at the mop and pail standing ready, at the
dishes stacked on the drainboard beside the sink.
"Oh, let them wait," she said, although there was no
one to hear in the empty house. Then she grabbed
up her old leather jacket and slammed the door on
the whole discouraging mess.

The cold air was dry, without the penetrating
chill Angela remembered from Philadelphia. There
was, she thought, searching for a word, an enthusiasm about the Vermont climate that was very
catching. No wonder she was filled with envy for
the skiers who overflowed from the village inns and
came to the Dodge farmhouse as paying guests.

They were so full of high spirits, so wind-tanned, so eager.

"You should learn to ski, Angie," they urged her. "At fourteen you'll learn quickly. It's such fun!"

But how could you ski without boots, without poles? They seemed to forget, these lucky people, that equipment cost money, and that money didn't grow on the bare branches of the sugar maples which bordered the farmhouse lane.

Money! Angela stood with clenched hands, hating the very word so violently that she forgot, for the moment, why she had come outside. Money was something she had never thought much about in Philadelphia, while her father was alive and paying the bills. It had never occurred to her to wonder how much food or fuel cost. It was never mentioned, that she could recall—but now! Now money—or the lack of it—seemed to dominate their lives. It had changed everything, ruined everything.

Resentment surged through her in a hot, engulfing flood. She had learned to let it drown the grief that had shadowed her ever since the tragic day of the air crash. Angela had convinced herself that it was better to feel cheated than to feel sick at heart. She could use resentment as a front. She could hide behind it. In her own way she could be brave.

Taking a long breath, she forced her mind back to the skis. They looked far more difficult to manage

than the snowshoes on which neighboring farmers
trudged across the snowy fields. Angela lowered
them to the floor, side by side, and slipped her
saddle shoes into the bindings, then bent her knees
and clutched imaginary poles.

How would it feel, she wondered, to swoop down
the mountainside? "Schussing," they called it—a
good word, a fast word. Would it be like having
wings on your feet? Like flying through snow?

She crouched a little, bending her ankles, leaning
forward, playing the old game of make-believe.
Now she was standing at the summit of a mountain.
Now she was pushing off with her poles. In her
imagination she could feel the rush of air against
her face as she swept down the dizzying descent.
Bending, straightening, swinging her slim hips in an
antic mimicry of a rhumba step, she no longer was
anchored to the level boards of the back porch.
She was a bird. She was flying free!

The rackety motor of a jeep suddenly jarred her
out of her daydream. Kicking off the skis quickly,
but too late, she glanced up to meet Dave Colby's
amused eyes.

"What are you doing, Angela? Posing for pic-
tures?" Dave cut the ignition and swung himself
out of the driver's seat. He was so tall and lanky
that Angela always thought of this process as un-
coiling. She'd watched him do it a dozen times
when he came to deliver the milk.

"Not me," she managed to retort. "I'd break the camera." It was a poor cliché, but she was embarrassed at being caught play-acting by an older boy. To cover her confusion, she bent and started to pick up the skis.

"They're for snow, you know, not board floors," Dave mentioned.

"They're broken," Angela announced, as though this settled everything.

"Where?"

Angela indicated the split tip. "Here. See? They're no good, Mr. Henderson said. He bought new ones."

Dave pulled the damaged ski toward him and examined it without speaking, and his silence made Angela edgy.

"I was just trying to find out how it would feel . . ." she stumbled on, "how it would seem . . ."

"You mean you don't know how to ski?"

The deep blue eyes looking up at Angela were candid, the question flat but not taunting. Yet she bit her lip. Was it because Dave was a junior and she a mere freshman in high school that he always seemed to catch her at a disadvantage? "You needn't act so surprised. We only moved here last summer," she reminded him.

"That's true." Dave spoke as though the point had escaped his notice, just as Angela herself would have escaped his notice if the Dodges hadn't lived along his delivery route. Although Burr and Burton was a small school, with only two hundred or so pupils, a skinny and rather apathetic new girl could easily get lost.

Running a finger along the split in the hickory, Dave traced it to a point just short of the binding. "A repair man would cut it here," he said, "and put on a whole new forepart. It would be strong enough to learn on, then."

"How much would it cost?"

The boy shrugged. "Five, ten bucks."

He might as well have mentioned a hundred. Angela took the skis and stood them back against the side of the house.

"They're a good make. It would be worth it."

"Maybe," Angela replied. She tried to sound disinterested, hoping to end the discussion, but Dave was just warming to the subject.

"You'd like skiing, I think. Are you good at sports?"

"Fair."

Angela sensed that Dave was appraising her as he would examine a promising colt, not as he would consider a girl. The girls Dave Colby really looked at were older and far prettier than she—girls like Jean Parker, a popular sophomore, who had outgrown her adolescent legginess and learned a few things about allure.

"How's your co-ordination?"

"Oh, Dave, I don't know! What difference does it make?"

The boy grinned, unabashed by the belligerent note in her voice. "Plenty," he told her. "So does nerve. You'll find out."

"Fat chance," Angela mumbled.

"What did you say?"

"Nothing."

Dave went around to the rear of the jeep, lifted out a couple of milk bottles, and handed them up to the porch. "Any extras?"

"No. The last of the week-enders just left. Mother drove them into Manchester."

"The highway's pretty slippery," Dave remarked, making conversation, which Angela was acute enough to recognize as an unusual trait in a Vermonter. He was still eying the skis.

"I could take 'em along and at least get a price for you," he suggested after a minute. "I know a guy in Peru who could do a job."

It was such an unexpected offer that Angela's eyebrows lifted in astonishment, but she shook her head. "Maybe some time," she said, clutching the milk bottles almost fiercely. "Some other time."

Dave looked puzzled. "Aren't you interested?" he asked. It didn't seem to occur to him that money was the stumbling block. Did all Vermonters, Angela wondered, think all out-of-state people were well off?

Of course! she wanted to shout. Haven't I watched and listened and yearned ever since there's been snow on the mountain? Instead, she countered with another question. "Why are *you* interested?"

Dave pulled his left ear thoughtfully and stood looking up at the girl on the porch, as though he couldn't make up his mind. The fading sun was lighting the sprinkling of freckles on Angela's short straight nose, the wind was brushing the hair back from her forehead, and she was holding herself tall and slim, with a certain spirit that Dave sensed without being able to express. "I think you've got the stuff, that's all," he said finally.

It was the first real compliment that Angela had ever been paid by a boy she admired. If she had stopped to analyze it, the praise might have been spoken of a dog or another boy. There was no reason to feel suddenly shy and shivery. "Thanks," she managed to mumble, then turned and fled into the kitchen without even a good-by. Kicking the door shut with her heel, she automatically carried the milk over to the refrigerator and put it away.

"The stuff." It was a lovely thought. It made her want to go out and conquer the world, and for a moment she felt as though she could. Then, with a jolt, she realized that she was back indoors, and that the sun was no longer shining through the window. Nothing else had changed in her absence except the hands of the clock, which now stood at

five instead of four-thirty. She gave a low whistle
of consternation and turned on the hot water.
Dishes first. At least she could *look* energetic when
her mother and Chip got home.

Nine-year-old Chip had been spending the afternoon with a friend down the road. He made friends,
Angela had noticed, as adventurously as he tackled
everything else in life, and today's companion had
a special aura, because he happened to be custodian
of a litter of six setter pups. Chip had been in on
the deal since the very day of their birth, now six
weeks past, and every afternoon on the way home
from school he stopped in to pay them a visit. On
Saturdays and Sundays he practically lived at the
Nickersons, ostensibly to play with his friend Sandy,
but actually to hang around the puppy pen and
coax one after another of the long-limbed babies
to come lick his hand.

He was talking about the pups when he came
tumbling out of the battered Ford station wagon
after his mother. "They *smell* so good!" he said as
he bounced through the kitchen door, and he wrin-
kled his nose appreciatively at the mere thought.

Janet Dodge smiled and nodded rather absently.
Her quick eyes took in the state of the kitchen, but
if she was disappointed she didn't say so. "The
roads are going to be really bad in another hour,"
she observed as she hung her coat on a peg. "It's
freezing fast."

"Maybe we won't have school tomorrow," suggested Chip hopefully. "Maybe the bus won't be able to get through."

"Never fear," retorted Angela.

Mrs. Dodge was rolling up her sleeves. "I'll finish up. You'd better get to your homework, Angie."

"What about supper?" asked Chip.

Angela knew that the week-end guests had practically cleaned out the refrigerator, but her mother appeared undisturbed. "I'll bring something on a tray and we'll eat in front of the fire a little later. Would you like that?"

Chip always liked that, as she well knew. So did Angela, for that matter. There was a coziness about it that made them seem all of a piece, like a family again, as if—

Deliberately she cut her own thought short. "Sure," she said, rather loudly, and crossed the room to dry her hands on the roller towel which hung on the back door.

"I'm hungry." Chip was complaining as he disappeared into the living room. Then, as an afterthought, he said, "Boy, you should see those pups eat!"

Angela was inclined to dawdle, even though she didn't pick up a towel. "Mr. Henderson left his old skis," she said after a minute or two.

"I noticed," murmured her mother. "He said they were split."

"They are, but they could be repaired," said Angela.

"Oh? We'll keep them around, then. Somebody
may want them." Plunging her cold hands into the
dishwater, Mrs. Dodge winced, then smiled. "If I
weren't so tired I'd shout, 'Hallelujah!'" she said
with satisfaction. "We took in forty-eight beautiful
dollars." She always said "we," not "I," and she
called Angela her junior partner, even though her
daughter recognized that the title was frequently
undeserved.

Angela, still thinking about the skis, said, "I guess
we needed it."

"Every penny. Now if this cold weather just
holds . . . !"

Angela crossed her fingers, knowing well what
her mother meant. If there was snow the skiers
would return. *If* there was snow! Over Christmas
there had been scarcely enough to cover the slopes,
and most of January had been rainy. In Manchester
and nearby Peru the innkeepers greeted one another glumly and went about their errands with
long faces. When there was no snow, the lifts on
Bromley Mountain could not run. Reservations
were canceled and motels and guesthouses were
empty. Mortgage money, food money—any kind of
money!—was hard come-by in Vermont when there
was no snow.

Finally there had come this white week end, too

late to save the season but nevertheless welcome, and to Mrs. Dodge a frail hedge against the fear that pursued her. Somehow, no matter what, she had to make a go of this project—but could she? When everything was so dependent on the weather, did she have a chance?

Angela, going up the winding stairs to the second floor in search of her schoolbooks, pondered the same question. One thing was certain. There was no use mentioning Dave's suggestion about the broken skis. Forty-eight dollars wouldn't stretch indefinitely, and the list of vital necessities was already long. Headed by shoes for Chip, who claimed that his toes were curled under alarmingly, it covered a dozen other mundane but indispensable things.

Skiing, Angela told herself, is out. There's no use dreaming about the impossible. Yet, settled on the living-room sofa with her books open on her lap, that was precisely what she did. Instead of doing her algebra assignment, she made a whole row of dollar signs and wondered what would happen if she should *find* the money somehow—lying in the road, perhaps dropped by a careless skier outside the General Store in Peru. Would it be hers to do with as she chose, or would she have a moral obligation to turn it over to her mother?

Darned if she would! Finders keepers. That was an unwritten rule of the game.

All right. She could get the skis repaired, now, with maybe a few dollars left over. She wondered where she could find secondhand boots. Because obviously it would be impossible to ski in saddle shoes. People were always talking about proper ankle support.

The dollar signs now stretched down the side of the sheet of lined paper which should have been filled with neatly written problems and answers by now. Angela sighed from boredom, rather than from any sense of guilt. She hated homework even more than she disliked housework. It was only when she was out of doors that she felt at all happy. "I'd rather chop wood or clean out the barn than do dishes," she'd told her mother just this morning. "I guess I should have been born a boy."

Mrs. Dodge had chuckled. "Then we could have called you Pete."

It was a joke between them: Angela's feeling that her name was completely unsuitable, that it was too feminine and namby-pamby for a girl as tall and big-boned as she was. "Probably every girl wishes she were a boy at some time or other," added Mrs. Dodge wisely. "But you'll outgrow it. Being a woman is something I wouldn't want to trade."

The remark recalled to Angela's mind another made by Mr. Henderson, who had patted her shoulder and thanked her on parting, as though he were a privileged friend of the family rather than a paying guest. "I'll be back soon!" he promised. "She's quite a woman, your mother. But I guess you know that."

He had been trying to tell her, Angela realized, that it was her mother's alchemy that made the skiers who overflowed from the inns around Bromley and found their way to the farmhouse want to return. Janet Dodge had a way with people, just as she had a way with cooking, or with decorating, or with making a blouse and skirt seem like a costume. She was bright and vigorous and capable, and the house she had furnished from bits and pieces of her disrupted life had charm and warmth.

"Ready for supper?"

As she walked into the living room now, with a heavy tray, her step was remarkably light. Angela got up to clear the bench in front of the fire, dumping the newspapers and magazines into Chip's lap.

"Hey!" he cried, letting them slide to the floor. "Oh, boy, French toast! My very favorite. Mmm."

"Come and get it," Mrs. Dodge invited them. She poured herself a cup of tea and settled back in the low rocker she liked best, kicking off her shoes and wriggling her toes as she held out her feet to the fire. Chip, meanwhile, was piling his plate with squares of the crisp toast, and pouring homemade maple syrup generously over all. Making private sounds of satisfaction, he arranged himself cross-legged on the floor with his supper on the hearth before him.

"Pour me a glass of milk, Angie?" he asked.

"Please," said Mrs. Dodge automatically.

"Please," Chip mumbled. "It's fresh milk, isn't it? We passed Dave on the road."

Angela didn't answer. She helped herself to a single piece of toast and carried it over to the couch, where she sat and ate it absent-mindedly. The stuff, she was thinking. He said I had the stuff.

"Tired, dear?" her mother asked after a few minutes.

She shook her head.

"Finish your homework?"

She shook her head again, without admitting that she hadn't even started. Her thoughts kept drifting back to the skis on the porch, and to Dave's suggestion. If she could only find a way, some possible way . . .

But Angela had no magic with which to conjure up dollars. The end result of all her dreaming was that she went into math class the next day without her assignment finished and stumbled through a history test unprepared. She passed Dave in the hall at three o'clock when she went for her coat and snow boots, but he was talking to Jean and didn't see her. All in all, it was a very depressing day.

When the old panel truck which served as a school bus passed Bromley, it was snowing at the top of the mountain, and a few bright-clad figures were discernible on the slopes; but to Angela they looked as unreal as men from Mars, while she herself had been brought down to earth with a dull thud. In the early dusk she trudged the last mile from the highway to the farm, staying out of the icy ruts, and crunching through the crust of snow to the soft powder beneath without the usual sense of satisfaction that she had in being alone in the silence and the mystery.

I will be more realistic, she told herself. I will try to do better. I will stop wishing for the moon.

There was a light in the kitchen and she could see her mother moving from stove to table and back again, getting supper. At the bottom of the back steps she stopped and kicked the loose snow off her boots, then cocked her head inquiringly. Something was different. Something was missing. Then she realized.

Mr. Henderson's skis were gone!

"THE SKIS!" Angela cried, bursting into the house. "Where are they? What have you done with them?"

Her mother turned from the wood stove, where she was stirring something in a pot, and said, "Why, nothing, dear. Aren't they there?"

Angela shook her head. She wasn't a girl who cried easily, but she felt close to tears tonight. "You —you don't think that they could have been stolen?"

"In Vermont? Nonsense."

"Then where are they?" Angela went through the dining room to the hall stairs and called, "Chip!"

"Yup," her brother replied from somewhere above, and Mrs. Dodge murmured, "That child sounds as though he'd been born here."

"Did you take Mr. Henderson's skis?"

"Nope," Chip replied in the same monosyllabic local manner.

"Then where can they be?" Angela asked no one in particular. "What can have happened to them?" She went outside again and peered around the porch, then picked up the milk bottles standing on the top step.

Dave!

"Do you suppose," she asked her mother in as casual a tone as possible, "that Dave could have taken them?"

"Why would he take them?" Janet Dodge questioned in mild surprise.

"He knows a man—in Peru—who could fix them, maybe."

"They'd be too short for Dave."

"I know."

Her mother's glance, suddenly sharp, told Angela that she recognized the implication behind this confession. Yet she waited a minute before she said, with careful patience, "Skiing is a rich man's sport, Angie. It isn't just the equipment—the boots and poles and parkas and pants. The lifts are expensive too, even at children's rates." She looked at her tall daughter with wistful affection. "And you won't be a child much longer, dear."

Angela didn't answer. Everything her mother said might be true, but she was prepared to discount it.

"There's the question of time, besides." Mrs. Dodge spoke slowly, as though she were thinking out loud. "Over week ends I really need you. I depend on you. I know you're young, and I don't blame you for being resentful, sometimes. But there's no help for it. I can't do it all alone."

There was nothing whining about Janet Dodge's tone. These were simple statements she was making, and Angela recognized them as such. She could have carried on the line of argument herself. The insurance her father had left, while it sounded substantial in a lump sum, provided pitifully little income in these times. The remodeling of the farmhouse for winter use had drained the last of their ready cash. Now they were scraping bottom. Only hard work and an abundance of paying guests could see them through.

Remembering her father, it seemed incredible to Angela that his death could have brought them to such a pass. He had such vitality, such daring and dash, that he had seemed indestructible, not only to his family but to himself. Even though his air-transport business was a risky one, and sometimes took him to the ends of the earth, he seemed to lead a charmed life. He always came back more robust, more full of vigor than ever. Until that fateful day . . .

Angela shook off the ghost riding her shoulder. What had her mother been saying? Something about needing her, now, over week ends. "I know," she murmured dully. "I know."

"Maybe some day," Mrs. Dodge suggested encouragingly, "maybe some day when we get on our feet and have a few dollars put aside—"

But Angela wouldn't let her finish. "Some day," she retorted grimly as she turned to leave the room, "never comes."

Of course, a moment later, she regretted her quick cruelty. She knew—how very well she knew!—that none of this was her mother's fault. But she had inherited her father's impatience, along with his nerve and sense of adventure. Some day, in her philosophy, should be tomorrow. Or, better still, now!

However, Angela stifled her curiosity concerning the skis for the rest of the evening. Her common sense told her that her mother was right. She let the subject drop, but it didn't prevent her wool-gathering, didn't keep her from leaning her head on her hands and looking into a Utopian future where everyone came equipped with skis at birth, just as they did with feet. Of course her Latin never got finished and her English composition was impossibly garbled, but Angela wasn't perturbed. School-work—pooh!

The next morning she rode into Manchester in a fidget. The other girls whom the bus picked up in Peru were discussing commonplace things like clothes and the coming basketball game with Rutland, but Angela didn't even pretend to be listening.

She was wondering where she might be most likely to run into Dave.

The Colbys lived in Manchester, and she knew he often got to classes quite late, because on several occasions, from the second-floor window, she had seen him sprinting down the curving drive leading to the old academy building which housed the school. If this was one of those days, she didn't stand a chance.

Did he bring his lunch, she wondered, or did he go home? Could she waylay him in the hall between bells, or was there a better chance of seeking him out during study period this afternoon?

"What do you think, Angie?" As the truck jounced along the curving road, Cora Fletcher, a serious girl with protruding teeth through which she had a habit of whistling, cut into her reverie.

"What do I think about what?" Not that I really care, Angela's expression seemed to say, as she turned her head in Cora's direction.

"Do you honestly think Rutland can beat us? With George Miller playing center and Dave Colby playing guard, I don't see how. They're both terribly tall. And good!"

"Does Dave play guard? I didn't know," Angela confessed, disregarding the question.

"Don't you ever come to a game?" asked Ellen Whipple, a small girl with white-blond hair and the perpetually surprised blue eyes of a kitten.

"She lives three miles t'other side of Peru. It's a fur piece," clowned Cora, laughing at her own deliberate colloquialism.

"It is, at that," agreed Angela, unperturbed.

"Still, you ought to have some school spirit," Ellen insisted. "Tell you what. If I can get you a ride Friday night I'll give you a call."

"Thanks," murmured Angela absent-mindedly. "That's very nice of you." Then suddenly she blurted out, "Can you ski?"

"Me?" Ellen squealed in unfeigned surprise. "Not on your life! I wouldn't be caught dead on those things—not the way I hate heights. Why I can't even go up in the church tower without feeling faint."

"I shouldn't think it would be the height that would get you," said Angela speculatively.

"What would it be, then?" Ellen's eyes became even more round.

"Speed. And the narrow margin for error."

Ellen tilted her head, considering, then gave up. "I don't understand what you're talking about," she said.

You wouldn't, Angela thought to herself. Here you have this whole great big beautiful state, these heavenly mountains, this exciting snow, and what do you do? Think about boys and basketball. She sat slumped down in the truck, letting the conversation pass over her head, recalling with nostalgia the friends with whom she had grown up at home. Betty would understand, or Gail, or Ruth. They had—what did they have? She searched for the phrase, then nodded as she found it—mental curiosity.

It didn't occur to Angela that her own mental curiosity was, at the moment, distinctly one-sided. Because lessons interested her even less than the snowy mountains interested Ellen Whipple, she dreamed and doodled through her morning classes and bluntly said, "I don't know," whenever she was called upon.

Vaguely, she was aware that her teachers were getting the impression that she was either dull or sullen. What did it matter? Compared with the up-to-date institution she had left, Angela considered Burr and Burton, an antiquated seminary converted into a high school to serve a large rural area, a stupid school anyway.

Every time she changed classes she looked for Dave Colby, but he seemed to have become invisible. He wasn't in his home room when she glanced in the door; he wasn't in the lunchroom; he wasn't in the gym. In the afternoon a general assembly was called for a visiting lecturer, and it was here that Angela at last caught a glimpse of him, seated several rows in front. She pushed and hurried to catch up with him on the way out, and at last at-

tracted his attention by reaching over an intervening pair of shoulders to touch him on the arm.

He turned. "Hi."

"Can I speak to you a minute?"

"Sure."

He stepped out of the crush, behind the double
doors, and Angela followed him. Without mincing
words she asked, "Did you take the skis?"

Dave looked disappointed for a moment, then
nodded. "I was going to surprise you. I thought
maybe you wouldn't miss them."

"I missed them," Angela murmured inadequately.

"Well," said Dave philosophically, "that's that."

"I've got to tell you," Angela went on, wringing
her hands, "I don't have any money."

Dave didn't seemed surprised. "I gathered that."

"Not *any*," Angela insisted. "Not two dollars—
not even *one!*"

"That makes us even," Dave told her, grinning.

"So-o . . ." Angela spread her hands and took a
long breath.

At this point a silence, almost tangible in its in-
tensity, fell between them. Angela recognized it
as a Vermont silence, typical of these boys and
men who prided themselves on their economy of
words. She waited for Dave to speak, while Dave
was waiting for her to finish her sentence. Finally
she giggled nervously. "This could go on forever,
I suppose."

The remark apparently meant nothing whatever to Dave. In any event he ignored it. "I thought I'd try to fix 'em up myself," he said finally. "Not so you could try anything fancy, mind you, but just so you could get out in that back pasture and learn to snowplow. You'd like that, wouldn't you?"

"Oh, yes!" Angela's heart was in her voice and in her melting brown eyes.

Dave smiled. "You can't go fast, understand. It would be dangerous."

"I understand." Angela nodded vigorously, her dark hair swinging against her cheeks.

"The split will only be glued, and the glue may not hold," the boy warned.

"I'll be careful."

"You don't *look* careful," said Dave unexpectedly. "I don't know why it is, but you don't look careful at all. If you were a horse, now, I'd say you were ready to bolt any minute. Any second! I'd say you were really on edge."

Angela laughed out loud. "I'm not a horse, Dave." For the first time she dared to glance at him impishly.

"Nope," the boy admitted, his grin returning. "I guess you're not."

He would have left then, but Angela said, "Wait! I just want to ask you one thing. What made you do it?"

"Do what?"

"Decide to fix the skis."

An expression of puzzlement which she had grown to recognize crept over Dave's face, and he began to pull at his ear. "Hanged if I know," he said reflectively. "It must have been that you had such a *wanting* look, and I kept remembering how I felt when I was about your age—"

A warning bell cut short his explanation and he hurried out into the hall. " 'By now," he muttered, then called over his shoulder as an afterthought, "at least the cow pasture will be better than skiing on the back porch!"

CHAPTER three

On Friday afternoon Angela had arranged to meet her mother at the one-room schoolhouse in Peru where Chip attended third grade. As she swung herself down from the bus and cut across the road to the path shoveled out through the snow, she might have been walking into a painting by Grant Wood or Grandma Moses. The bottle-green shingle building was shaped like a salt box and trimmed with white. A square steeple housed the school bell, and this, combined with small-paned windows rounded at the top, gave it the air of a miniature country church.

Chip was waiting in the empty room he normally shared with about thirty other children, from seven to fifteen years old. He showed Angela around proudly, stopping at the desk he was allowed to use with another third-grader and pointing out the gold

star on a crayon drawing posted above the blackboard.

"See that? It's mine!"

Angela squinted up at several blobs of rusty red.
"Hot dogs?" she asked.

"Don't be a dope." Chip was not amused.
"They're just-born setter puppies." He cocked his
head critically. "Or maybe one day old."

"Are they *that* smooth and shiny?" Angela looked
dubious.

"Sure," Chip said with superior wisdom. "You
ought to see them now, though. Boy, oh, boy!"

"Are they fat?" Angela asked, to make conversation.

"Not too," Chip said warily. "All puppies are fat,
sort of. Or else they aren't healthy. These are very
healthy. They've had their first temper shots."

"*Distemper*," corrected Angela, turning to the
window to hide her smile. She could see her mother
coming up the path, and thought she looked especially pretty, with an old red cap pulled over her
short curly hair and the collar of her coat turned
up against the cold. Her cheeks were pink and her
step was so springy that Angela knew she must be
excited about something and wondered what could
have happened that would make her look so enthusiastic and young.

"Ready, children?" Mrs. Dodge asked a moment
later as she pushed open the door. "I've got the

wagon simply *loaded* with groceries. It's going to
be another busy week end. Ten reservations so far!"

Angela stifled a groan. Is that all? she wanted to
ask, but restrained herself. With one part of her
mind—the almost-grown-up part—she knew that this
was indeed cause for celebration, but with a rebel-
lious childishness she dreaded the long hours of
drudgery. It flashed through her consciousness that
even if Dave dropped off the mended skis today or
tomorrow, she'd have no opportunity to try them
out. Counting their own family there would be thirteen people to feed. Thirteen, in itself, was an un-
lucky number! As Chip dragged his mother over
to admire his painting of the puppies, Angela
started dispiritedly toward the car.

It had never occurred to her—foolishly enough!—
that if snow conditions were good the house would
be jam-packed with skiers, and that time of her own
would be at a premium. Bedding and feeding a
large group of people took more than her mother's
admirable organization. It took hard physical labor,
and one pair of hands just wasn't enough.

Riding three-in-the-front-seat along the highway,
Angela considered her younger brother speculatively. Could he be trained to do more? At the
moment, chattering about his beloved setters, he
seemed little more than a puppy himself, capable
of carrying in the firewood and doing small short

chores, but certainly not ready to assume any real responsibility.

"Could you drop me off at Nickersons'?" he was asking now. "I'll walk the rest of the way home. I don't mind."

"But why, dear? Sandy's gone to his aunt's for the week end," Mrs. Dodge reminded him.

Chip squirmed between his mother and his sister. He's feeling hemmed in, Angela realized with reluctant sensitivity, and she wasn't surprised that he stammered a little when he explained, "I'd sort of like to say good night to the dogs."

"That's a lot of foolishness. You can see them tomorrow," she felt impelled to say, and immediately wondered why she had spoken. Was it because she wanted to make him grow up as she was growing up, through being hurt, through being denied, through being obstructed? She knew in her heart that seeing the dogs tomorrow wouldn't be the same at all, that Chip was full of *wanting* as she was, but that their focus was different. After all, he was only nine years old.

Her mother, who seemed to be giving the request consideration, turned off the highway into the dirt road which led up the mountain toward home. "Will you promise to be in before dark?" she asked after a minute.

Chip nodded vigorously. "Cross my heart."

When they pulled up before the Nickersons' gate

they could hear the puppies yapping, and a smile of
pure delight settled on Chip's face. He slid between
his sister and the dashboard and slithered out the
door like a young eel. "Listen to 'em!" he cried.
"Just listen to 'em! Aren't they great?"

But when he arrived home three quarters of an
hour later, he had been crying. Angela, who was
helping her mother put away groceries and prepare
vegetables in the kitchen, instantly recognized the
grubby streaks which in books were always politely
called tearstains. He muttered a mechanical greet-
ing, and went straight through the kitchen to the
dining room, and then on upstairs, and when he
came down again his face and hands were unaccus-
tomedly clean.

For a few minutes he stood around, saying nothing, and then he burst out with it. "Mr. Nickerson
sold two of my puppies! And he never even told me.
I never even got a chance to see them first!" Fresh
tears spilled over and he stood with his hands
clenched and feet apart, furious and hurt.

Mrs. Dodge turned from the lettuce she was washing. "But they weren't your puppies, Chip."

"They almost were! I even saw two of them
born." His knuckles brushed the angry tears from
his cheeks.

Mrs. Dodge snatched a quick glance at the clock,
but her voice was gentle and unhurried. "You love
them, I know, but the puppies belong to Penny, and

Penny belongs to the Nickersons. You're not thinking straight, Chip."

"I don't care!" Chip wailed. Then he flared up.
"I—I hate him, the old goat!"

Angela assumed, quite correctly, that he was referring to Mr. Nickerson; but there came a distrac-
tion, at that moment, in the familiar racket made by
Dave Colby's jeep. She hurried to the door, and her
heart gave a quick leap.

"He has them!" she cried to no one in particular.
"He has my skis!"

"*Your* skis! *Your* puppies!" Janet Dodge put her
hands to her head in consternation. "Heaven help
me until the two of you grow up."

But Angela, already out on the porch, didn't hear
her. "Is it fixed?" she was asking Dave. "Will the
glue hold?"

"I don't know," he admitted. "My pop says it's
not likely. As a matter of fact, he doesn't think it's
going to be very safe—"

"Sh!" Angela warned. "Don't let Mother hear
you." She took the skis and leaned them against the
house far back in the corner of the porch, then
stroked them appreciatively. "I'll be careful—honestly I will. I'll only use them out back on our little
hill. I won't go on any real slopes."

"You'd better not," Dave warned grimly. "You'd
be liable to kill yourself." He stood looking so un-
decided that Angela tried to distract him.

"Dave—"

"Huh?"

"Would you—sometime when you're coming out this way—could you come early and teach me a few things?"

Dave hesitated, then agreed with a wry grin. "I guess I'd better, if I don't want you to break a leg."

From the back door Mrs. Dodge called, "Better leave six quarts of milk, please."

"You must have a full house," Dave said as he handed the bottles up to Angela.

"We're about to."

"You won't have much time to practice this week end," he added in a teasing tone. "Probably just as well."

But he reckoned without Angela's excitement at the knowledge that there they stood, the two long shafts of hickory, waiting and ready to be tried. She went to bed full of an intemperate compulsion, and lay staring wide-eyed at the moon, which swept across her room like a searchlight and glistened on the white snow outside.

When she could stand it no longer she crept out of bed, quiet as a cat, pulled jeans over her pyjamas, and slipped her feet into a pair of heavy woolen socks. In the hall a sweater hung on a peg, so she caught it up in passing and silently slipped downstairs.

The problem of footgear was paramount. She had brought along her saddle oxfords, but she knew they'd never do. Finally she remembered her mother's abandoned jodhpur boots, and delved into the coat closet after them, shivering nervously every time the door gave a squeak.

Gloves. A scarf. She was ready. Like a shadow she emerged on the back porch. Trying to walk on tiptoe was next to impossible, but she put one foot in front of the other cautiously. Silence was important.

Once she was down the steps, her heart began to thump less desperately. " 'The moon on the breast of the new-fallen snow,' " she said to herself. What a picture! What a night! A single pine stood inky-black against the hillside, and the shadows of the bare maples and birches lay blue against the white blanket. Angela felt like a sprite, a snow nymph, insubstantial, completely outside of this world.

She felt that way only for a moment, however, because the skis were awkward and she didn't know how to carry them properly, although she had watched many a girl swing them up over her shoulder as though they were featherweight. Holding them across her chest in both arms, she trudged up the snow-packed path to the barn, where she would be out of sight from her mother's bedroom and comparatively free from the possibility of detection.

Then, placing the slender shafts of wood side by side on a level place, she tried them on.

At once it was apparent that the jodhpur boots had no ridges cut in the heels to grip the bindings, but Angela snapped the steel springs in place anyway and lifted one foot tentatively. "Heavens!" she murmured aloud. Never had she dreamed that they could feel so long and awkward. The shovel tips stretched half her length ahead and the tails, when she turned and looked back, seemed equally far behind.

Sliding one ski forward, she brought the other up and past it, then realized why she felt strangely detached. She had no poles! But there was a slick, smooth feel to the surface of the skis on the snow that made her breath catch sharply. Almost—almost!—she could imagine what it would be like to really glide.

The path dropped a little toward the house—not sharply, but so that the tips of her skis were, for a moment, in the air. Then, as Angela leaned forward, testing the sensation of crouching, she felt herself take off downhill.

Instinctively she did the right thing. She kept her ankles bent, her skis parallel, the tips together. She was moving fast for one wonderful moment, and then she saw a snowbank looming ahead and toppled sideways as she tried to swerve.

One ski stuck up in the air; the other raced down-hill without her, but it didn't matter. She lay in the snow and smiled up at the unblinking moon.

This was going to be wonderful—wonderful!—beyond anything she had ever known!

CHAPTER four

BEFORE ANYONE WAS UP the next morning, Angela went out to the barn and found two abandoned brooms. She sawed off the handles to the approximate length of ski poles and drilled holes through the rounded ends. To these she attached loops of rope which she could slip over her wrists, but the snow rings at the bottom of the poles defeated her. She could think of no way to improvise such gadgets, although she knew their importance. They would keep the tips, which she had managed to sharpen to crude points, from sinking too deeply into the snow.

"Angela!"

"Coming, Mother." She slid down the path to the back door. The kitchen was aromatic with coffee and bacon odors, and the four guests who had arrived the night before were already seated at the

44

breakfast table. Mrs. Dodge didn't waste time on questions. "There's a plate of buttered toast in the oven," she told her daughter. "Please carry it in."

There were bacon and eggs to serve, coffee cups to be refilled. Then the skiers were off in a rush and a bustle, congratulating one another on the weather, talking about snow conditions on the various slopes. Mrs. Dodge waved good-by to them from the back porch, calling, "Have a good day! See you for dinner." Genial and smiling, she was the perfect hostess, and her guests all shouted satisfied farewells. But Angela, clearing the table and stacking the plates for washing, couldn't quell a feeling of envy. If only she could be going too!

She raced through the morning chores, finishing the breakfast dishes in half her usual time, preparing beds for the six guests still to come, and bringing down sleeping bags to stow in the hall closet for herself and Chip, so that they could "make do" in the small study off the living room. Her mother, stirring up brown bread in the kitchen, was humming a current song hit, the sun was shining, and the house looked especially hospitable and warm, but Angela kept glancing out of the window.

"Is there anything else for me to do?" she asked as soon as she decently could.

Janet Dodge put a kettle of water on the wood stove and said, "Not for the moment, Angie. You sound impatient. Is there something special on your mind?"

Angela nodded. "I'd like to go outside for a while," she admitted, "and fool around with those skis."

Her mother frowned. "You haven't any boots, dear. Or poles. I don't want to be a spoilsport, but can't you see it's out of the question?" She paused helplessly, then added, "You could hurt yourself. You could break a leg."

"I'll be careful," Angela promised. Then, to forestall a further argument, she explained hastily, "I just want to *play* with them really, out in the back pasture. I just want to find out how it would feel."

Mrs. Dodge sighed and shook her head. "Be back in an hour," she said, capitulating. "And don't try anything foolish. Promise now!"

Angela grabbed her mother around the waist in a quick hug of appreciation. "I promise." Then she hurried out to the barn for her crude poles.

Chip, who was dawdling over his only chore, the assembling of firewood, was inspecting his sister's handiwork critically. "What are these s'posed to be?" he asked.

Angela explained willingly enough. "But they need rings at the bottom," she admitted. "Got any good ideas?"

Chip shook his head. "What you need are *real* poles," he said firmly. "These are heavy old things."

"Thanks a bushel." Angela took the broomsticks from him. "Buy me a pair, will you," she suggested, "next time you're in Manchester?"

"I haven't got any money," Chip retorted, uncertain about the sarcasm.

"Haven't you?" his sister asked in mock surprise. "Funny thing, neither have I."

This ended the interchange, although Angela half expected Chip to follow her up to the pasture, forgetting that he kept a practically permanent rendezvous with the Nickerson pups. It was a relief, naturally, to be able to fool with the mended skis and her makeshift equipment without her brother's inevitable comments. She felt completely safe from discovery or interference, because the pasture was hidden behind the house, and because her mother was too busy to be either curious or greatly concerned.

But the hour, captured so neatly out of the very heart of the morning, proved woefully inadequate after all. First Angela had to stamp down a run in the snow, and again and again the bindings slipped off the heels of the jodhpur boots and the skis skidded away downhill. Again and again she retrieved them, and fastened them on as best she could. The broomsticks, used as poles, were ridiculous. They plunged through the snow into the earth and offered no resistance at all.

At the end of the time Angela was almost ready

to admit complete and total defeat. She was per-
spiring and frustrated and breathless, and she could
have thrown the borrowed riding boots into the
stove. Remembering her anticipation, which had
sustained her during the entire week, she felt
drained and subdued. Maybe her mother was right
after all. Maybe there were too many odds against
her. Maybe she'd better just plain give up.

There was a plate of sandwiches in the center
of the kitchen table when she trudged back to the
house, and her mother was ladling split-pea soup
into bowls. Chip was already seated, a book open
beside his paper napkin. He looked up and greeted
his sister with more interest than usual.

"Ever read *Hans Brinker?*" he asked.

"Seems to me I must have. Something about a
poor Dutch boy and some silver skates?" Angela
kept her voice even and conversational with a determined effort. She didn't want to betray her emotion,
didn't want either Chip or her mother to see that
her hands were trembling, didn't want them to make
light of her disappointment, which was almost too
great to bear.

"That's right! But before he got his *good* skates—
the ones he won races with—he had homemade
wooden ones. Did you know that?"

"I don't remember," Angela confessed, pushing
her damp hair back from her forehead and pulling
up a chair. "What are you driving at?"

Chip chuckled. "I was thinking of your ski poles."

Angela's chin rose belligerently. "So?"

"Maybe a rich lady will come along and give you money for some real poles," Chip suggested, and Angela saw that instead of intending to tease her he was actually hopeful, half convinced that such a miracle could occur, even in Vermont.

But Angela shook her head and said slowly, "Those things only happen in storybooks."

"Do they?" the child asked, his eyebrows drawing together in disillusionment. "Are you sure?"

It wasn't a question that had to be answered, because at that moment his mother bent and rumpled his hair affectionately. "Nobody's sure of anything," she said out of tragic experience, and yet with no trace of bitterness. "In this wonderful world of ours anything can happen. You keep on believing that!"

Chip settled back in his chair, munching a sandwich, and his expression grew dreamy again. To Angela he looked as though he were gazing into the future—an impossibly attractive future, and she would have been willing to wager it was largely peopled by dogs.

In a way it would be nice to be Chip's age again, full of high hope, ready to look on the bright side of life with any encouragement at all. But she wondered whether it was right for her mother to encourage him to be so optimistic. Maybe, in the long run, he would be happier if he expected nothing, because nothing was apt to be what he'd get.

She picked up half a sandwich, then put it back on the plate. "I'm not really hungry," she confessed. The mood of depression grew, reached its inevitable climax, then was routed by an unexpected idea. "Mother," she asked suddenly, "would you mind if I had ridges cut in the heels of those old jodhpur boots of yours?"

"Why?"

"So my bindings would hold better."

Janet Dodge looked puzzled. "Bindings?"

"On the skis. They keep slipping off. It wouldn't hurt the boots at all, honestly."

"I could cut them," Chip offered, "with my saw."

"Cut them in leather?" his mother asked dubiously, then spoke to her daughter, "I think you'd better take them to the shoemaker in Manchester."

Of course there was no opportunity to do this until Monday, but even so it was a ray of light in Angela's private gloom. She carried the boots to school on the bus, took them to the repair shop in the afternoon, and explained to the puzzled owner of the store exactly what she had in mind.

Mistrustfully, the man followed her bidding, and charged her twenty-five cents. As the girl turned away from the counter, he shook his head and offered a sensible suggestion. "It's ski boots you need,

Miss, beggin' your pardon. Those is for ridin' a horse."

Nevertheless, the ridges were an improvement. Although it was almost dark when Angela reached home, she took them out back to her homemade run and tried them out. Now, instead of losing a ski every few seconds, she could keep them on for minutes at a time. Running down the gentle slope, attempting a snowplow, she began to recapture the excitement that had filled her that first moonlit night. This was something she wouldn't give up. This was something she *had* to do!

The next afternoon Chip surprised her with a present, which he presented the instant she entered the house. Out of two round ends from a Crisco can he had fashioned a pair of snow rings for her poles. They were of questionable strength, and the method by which he had secured them to the broomsticks left a great deal to be desired, but Angela was touched, and thanked him warmly, promising to try them out at once.

She was in the back pasture a few minutes later, testing them on a gentle incline, when Dave Colby ambled around the corner of the house.

As he neared the fence he squinted, then peered in astonishment which turned quickly to amusement, and burst out with a frank, uninhibited guffaw. "You ought to be on television!" he hooted. "You'd make all the other comics look sick."

Angela snowplowed to a stop almost in front of him, well aware that she must make a ridiculous picture in the pleated plaid school skirt she hadn't bothered to change, heavy wool socks designed to be worn with Bermuda shorts, the incongruous jodhpur boots, and the broomstick poles with Chip's rings of tin glinting like flying saucers in the sunset. "If you hear of any jobs going begging, I'm open to an offer," she said with a wry grin. "Especially if there's a little money around." Then she held forth the broomsticks for Dave's inspection. "I could use some new poles."

"You could also use some boots," commented Dave, leaning on the fence and staring down at Angela's peculiarly shod feet. "Girl, you'll break your neck in those."

"Watch me!" challenged Angela, turning to angle up the slope with a side step which emphasized the loose fit of the unfortunate boots. Five minutes later she called from the top, "Tell me if my ankles and knees are right!" Then she shoved off and schussed down to snowplow once more directly in front of Dave.

The boy whistled softly. "Not bad," he said, "considering your equipment. "You've got the idea of keeping your belt buckle comfortably low and forward."

"My belt buckle? What's that got to do with it? As a matter of fact, I'm not even wearing a belt."

Dave laughed. "It's just an expression. Wait a minute," he suggested. "I'll get my skis and show you how to traverse."

"Traverse," Angela repeated, as she watched the boy walk back toward the jeep parked out of sight around the corner of the house. "Traverse." She was going to have to learn a whole new vocabulary, a different language, but she didn't feel in the least abashed.

Dave worked with her for nearly half an hour, until the sun sank behind Styles Mountain and the air grew suddenly chill. He taught her how to edge her skis in toward the hill, with the uphill ski forward. He showed her how her downhill shoulder could balance the forward thrust of the uphill hip. She could feel the skis evenly pressed into the snow, with the lower ski carrying a little more weight than the other, and she knew instinctively that this was right, because she felt comfortable and in command. Brushing off the snow after an occasional tumble, she disregarded the cold and ignored the inadequacy of her skirt. She would have kept right on following Dave's directions, so intense was her concentration, so acute her desire to learn.

Mrs. Dodge came to the back door as Dave tossed his skis back into the jeep. "Can you take time for a cup of hot chocolate?" she asked, but the boy shook his head.

"Give me a rain check, please, ma'am. I've got

ten other calls to make before I knock off for supper." He bade Angela a quick good-by. "You'll do all right," he promised, "but you've got to get yourself some boots somehow." He glanced at the jodhpur boots with infinite masculine disdain. "You'll never get past the snow-bunny class in those."

Angela accosted her mother immediately. "You heard what he said."

"I heard."

"*How* can I get some ski boots?" she implored. "I've *got* to have them. Maybe I can find some baby-sitting jobs. Maybe I can work week ends down at Bromley in the cafeteria!"

"I need you here, week ends," said Janet Dodge flatly, although Angela could tell by her mother's expression that it cost her an effort.

"Then pay me!"

"Angela!" Distress pinched the corners of Mrs. Dodge's mouth.

Standing adamant, with her legs slightly apart, her chin up, Angela said, "I don't care! I've got to have boots and I *will*, somehow, some way, and soon!" She stamped through the door into the dining room, then whirled around as an idea struck her. "Why can't we sell some of these precious antiques?" she almost shouted. "What's furniture, anyhow? We can sit on packing boxes if we have to. I can study at the kitchen table instead of at a Chippendale desk. I'd rather ski!"

The outburst was so frenzied, so completely un-expected, that Mrs. Dodge stood quite still, without speaking, for several seconds. Then, in a voice determinedly calm, she said, "Angela, there are two things we won't do. We won't touch principal, unless there is a real emergency, and we won't sell our inherited furniture unless we are actually hungry." With her chin raised even higher than her daughter's, she added, *"Perhaps not even then!"*

CHAPTER { *five*

THERE WAS FRESH SNOW for the Washington's Birthday week end, which was festival time at Bromley. The waiting lines were long at each of the lifts, and every ski lodge and motel was jammed with capacity crowds.

Angela and Chip again resorted to sleeping bags and Mrs. Dodge gave up her bedroom and spent two nights on the living-room couch. There were slalom and downhill races, and a pretty snow queen marched smiling between crossed poles, but none of this did Angela see. Her mother had the house filled to overflowing, with extra people coming from rooms in nearby farmhouses for breakfast and dinner, and there wasn't a time when Angela could be spared.

She made beds and peeled potatoes and emptied ash trays and set tables and washed dishes and listened with both ears to the skiing talk. She soon learned to cull the experts from the novices. These skiers talked about the Corkscrew trail, the Peril and the Blue Ribbon, argued about the merits of various waxes, and felt strongly about the Austrian versus the French technique. They used all sorts of strange terms, which Angela stored away in her memory so that she could ask Dave about them—terms like *ruade, parallel christie, counterrotation,* and *windup.* Many of them had skied in Europe, and they discussed Davos and Klosters and Kitz-buhel, faraway, romantic places of which Angela had never heard.

To a man—to a woman!—they seemed to her to be glamorous, exciting people, full of daring and full of verve. The fact that they were utterly self-ab-sorbed didn't bother her. She accepted their devo-tion to the sport without question. If she were in their place, her allegiance would be complete.

Only once, during the long week end, did Angela have a chance to get out on her practice slope, which was covered with new snow and therefore doubly inviting. It was late on the afternoon of the Monday holiday, and many of the skiers had al-ready packed and left for the long drive back to New York. A few, from nearby Albany, still re-mained, and this carload happened to return from Bromley just as Angela was stowing her gear away on the back porch.

One of the women, noticing the jodhpur boots into which she had tucked the cuffs of an old pair of blue jeans, stopped and looked thoughtful. "I have an old pair of ski boots at home that might fit you," she said. "Would you like me to look them up?"

"Would I!" Angela's heart was in her voice.

"I'm not too sure of the size. Do you remember, Larry?"

Larry, whose last name was Townsend, did not remember, but he said to his wife, "Send them along anyway. If they don't fit, maybe she can trade with somebody or other." He shook a warning finger in Angela's direction. "You shouldn't be risking your neck on those doggoned things!"

"They're not very practical," Angela admitted, then flashed Mrs. Townsend a smile which said more than the words which followed. "You don't know how grateful I'd be!"

"If they fit."

Angela nodded. "They've just *got* to fit."

From the next day on, she rode a rising tide of impatience. She ran home from the crossroads where the school bus dropped her and arrived breathless at the farmhouse, to burst through the door and call anxiously, "Did the mailman bring a package for me?"

Her mother's answer was repeatedly negative. "Darling, you're overanxious. It takes parcel post several days to get here. Besides, you can't expect Mrs. Townsend to have remembered to get the boots off first thing Monday morning. She has other things to do."

"When do you *think* they might come, then?"

Janet Dodge gave a questioning shrug. "Sometime next week, perhaps."

"She wouldn't forget, would she?" Angela tried to remember whether Mrs. Townsend had looked at all vague.

"I don't think so. Be patient."

But how could she be patient when the thing was so important? How could she lose herself in the routine of schoolwork when the snow was just right and the hills were beckoning?

Even the air tasted of expectation! On Thursday afternoon, as Angela hurried home in the early dusk, she felt curiously alive and excited, as she used to feel on Christmas Eve. Everything about her seemed vivid. The bare trees made fascinating patterns against the silver sky, and the white snow bore the sharply cut signatures of deer which had cut down through the birch woods and crossed the road on their way to the brook.

"Hi, Angie." A small voice spoke so unexpectedly that Angela started.

"Hello, Chip? Where did you come from?"

There was no need to answer, because a nod could indicate the direction of the Nickersons' shed.

"They're all gone but one," the child announced mournfully.

Angela knew that she should say something sensible and comforting. "I hope they all got good homes," she murmured, knowing just how unsatisfactory this must sound. Glancing at Chip's pinched, sad little face, she understood why her mother was worried about him. Mrs. Dodge was afraid Chip would grieve himself sick before the final wrench came and the last of the puppies was sold.

The boy shrugged but didn't answer. He had fallen into step beside his sister and was trudging along with sagging shoulders, as though he were very tired.

"The mother will still be left," Angela suggested after a few minutes. "Maybe she'll have another litter next year."

Next year. She knew, even as she spoke, that next year would sound as faraway as the moon to Chip. *Next year!* Such a pompous, foolish remark to make.

Yet she couldn't take it back, and could think of no direct, honest way to approach her brother. It was as though she had drifted, without realizing it, into an adult world where such remarks were commonplace, where people spoke inanities to children, because wisdom seemed too harsh.

"It wouldn't be the same," Chip muttered, and

kicked at a stone which protruded through the hard-packed snow.

Angela was aware that this reply was intended to close the conversation, that she had earned his contempt after he had offered his confidence; yet how could she have done otherwise? What was there, actually, to say? She frowned, sorry for him and ashamed of her own ineptitude, yet vaguely annoyed that her mood of expectation had been broken. "Let's run!" she suggested, trying to pick up the fragments. "I'll beat you to the porch steps!"

Of course she couldn't. Chip, fleet as a yearling, easily outstripped her. But he ran without zest this evening and took no pleasure in his victory. At dinner he toyed with his food, pushing the potatoes around on his plate and finally begging off.

"I don't feel too good," he said to his mother, and went off to sit in front of the living-room fire and mope.

Mrs. Dodge sighed. "I'll be glad when this passionate love affair is ended," she confessed in a whisper. "Poor baby. I hate to see him hurt."

"It's his own fault," Angela said almost angrily, to hide her secret understanding. "He shouldn't be so intense."

Mrs. Dodge chuckled. "Look who's talking! You and Chip don't just acquire hobbies. You launch forth on crusades."

As she sat through a dull math period the next

morning, Angela remembered this remark, impressive because it was so true. Just a few weeks ago she had thought little or nothing about skiing, but now it was a burning interest which consumed most of her waking thoughts.

Skiing—and Dave.

Yes, she admitted to herself, the two were inevitably linked in her mind, even though she put Dave second deliberately. Because he had been so helpful about repairing the skis and so kind as to teach her the rudiments of the sport, Angela had developed for Dave a sort of hero worship. She kept seeking out his face in assembly and manufacturing reasons to speak to him in the hall.

Of course, as soon as possible, she had told him about the promised boots. Dave whistled appreciatively and made a circle of his thumb and forefinger, indicating approval, but he didn't pause to discuss the matter. This, as Angela well knew, was because she had approached him in school. At Burr and Burton Dave Colby was a big man, too important to be found chatting with a freshman as insignificant as Angela Dodge.

This didn't especially disturb her. She accepted it as she accepted any other incontrovertible fact. At the farmhouse Dave might lend her an ear and his encouragement, but at school he was taken up with girls like Jean Parker, who really merited attention. Angela was just by-the-way.

Of course, dreamed Angela, as she stared unseeing at the algebraic equation on the blackboard, some day this might change. Some day, when she was one of the experts at Bromley, when she could rest on her poles at the top of the Corkscrew and be queen of all she surveyed, then Dave Colby might give her a second glance! This happy time seemed very far away, yet strangely near, because when Angela couldn't act she could build remarkably substantial castles in the air.

"Angela Dodge, how would you solve this problem?"

Dumped peremptorily from her magic carpet, Angela stammered, "I—I'm not sure, Mr. Carter."

"You mean you don't know? In mathematics it is either one thing or the other, black or white. There are no shades of gray."

"I guess I don't know, then."

Mr. Carter, who was sparse-haired and thin, sighed and peered at Angela through his bifocals. "I should like to mention once more," he said primly, "that mathematics is not a class through which you can sit and daydream. Mathematics can teach you something, young lady. It can teach you obedience to authority. It can teach you to follow the rules, and even if you do not become a genius in this field that is a valuable lesson to learn."

"Yes, Mr. Carter," murmured Angela, embarrassed to be the focus of attention but not really impressed by the lecture.

"Very well! Now then, Ellen Whipple?"

Ellen knew the solution. In spite of the fact that Ellen looked as soft as a kitten and spoke in a high-pitched baby's voice, she always knew the answers. Angela stared at her disgustedly. Show-off, she thought. Teacher's pet.

Yet at the same time she recognized she was being unfair. Because she herself was bored with schoolwork, because she was otherwise absorbed, was no reason to malign Ellen. Pulling herself together, Angela tried to pay attention, but the problem the class was considering was quite beyond her. She had let herself drift too far behind.

Riding back to Peru on the bus that afternoon, she made a pact with her own conscience. If the ski boots had arrived, she would do her homework right away, this very evening, so that she wouldn't be tempted to put it off indefinitely and then go to school on Monday unprepared.

"I promise," she whispered, and in imagination crossed her heart. It didn't occur to her that it was childish to try to propitiate fate. Since coming to Vermont she had drifted into all sorts of odd habits, because she had been forced to live so much within herself.

Now, once more, she swung herself down from the truck and turned into the home road eagerly.

Today she had every right to expect that the boots would have arrived. She ran until her heart pumped wildly and her side ached, walked until she could catch her breath, then ran once more.

It was there! A package so big and bulky that it seemed to occupy the entire kitchen table. Angela fell on it eagerly.

"For me?" she asked, even though she was sure.

Her mother nodded, and brought a knife as Angela began to pull at the cord which bound it. "Don't be so impatient, darling," she said.

"Impatient!" Impatience wasn't the word. Angela tore and tugged at the wrapping. Bless Mrs. Townsend! "She did remember," she murmured thankfully. Bless the entire Townsend family for having saved the boots until the time came when they could give them to someone as needy as herself! Angela lifted them out of the carton with fingers that trembled, undismayed that the boots had seen extremely hard wear and were scuffed and scraped.

"Goodness, they're heavy!" she breathed, and the remark sounded like a hymn of praise.

Janet Dodge smiled and dried her hands, which were as rough and red as a man's, in spite of the almond-shaped nails, which were still beautiful. She came and stood by the table while Angela kicked off her snow boots and loafers. "Should you try them with heavy socks?" she asked.

But Angela couldn't wait. She picked up the

right boot and edged her cold toes into it, tugging
with both hands as she bore down on her heel.
The tangled laces were too tight. She had to loosen
them. Then she yanked at the tongue, because it
seemed to be binding. Standing, she strained on
the boot with both hands and stamped anxiously.
"They're a little bit stiff," she murmured, but already
the bitter truth was dawning. Her heel just wouldn't
go down.

In the miserable moment of realization she looked
up at her mother, stricken. "They're too small."
Then, appalled by her own bald statement, she
tugged again until her cheeks grew crimson with
the effort and her foot felt as though it were being
crushed in a vise. "Oh, Mother, they can't be, but
they are!"

Mrs. Dodge picked up the left boot and measured
it with Angela's loafer, sole to sole. The comparison
made fear a certainty.

There was nothing to say, no word of comfort
that could have done anything but flick the wound
of Angela's disappointment. She fought the hot
tears which filled her eyes, and gritted her teeth in
desperation. Why hadn't she hedged her anticipation with Mrs. Townsend's warning that the boots
might not fit? Why did she count on things so
much?

"You might," her mother was saying gently, "see

if you can trade them with some girl at school. You might put a notice on the bulletin board."

"People's feet grow. They don't shrink. Who'd want to get rid of a big pair of boots for smaller ones?"

There was no answer, no hopeful answer. Mrs. Dodge stood mute.

Then, as though the very silence in the kitchen were an entrance cue, a new actor in the domestic drama appeared on stage. Chip, who had arrived unheard, threw open the back door and stepped into the room, an expression of pure bliss on his face and a silky, copper-colored setter puppy clasped firmly in both arms.

"He's mine!" he said, and no father gazing at a first-born son could have been more proud. "Mr. Nickerson gave him to me." Tears of wonder and joy stood in his eyes, and, to cover such unmanly emotion, he bent his head and buried his face in the setter's glossy coat.

For a long moment Mrs. Dodge was too surprised to speak, but Angela could tell that her mother was filled with conflicting emotions. The problem of the boots was no longer paramount. Here was a real poser—alive and breathing and wagging his tail!

The puppy was adorable. There was no doubt about it! Loose-jointed and leggy, it squirmed happily in Chip's loving arms. But even as Angela's

heartstrings twanged, her mind stiffened. This was
no time to take on an added responsibility, another
mouth to feed, another youngster to raise. Why,
compared to a pair of ski boots, the cost would be
fabulous! There would be the final distemper shots,
cod-liver oil, the inevitable puppy illnesses and accidents and veterinarian bills.

She could remember Sherry, the cocker spaniel
with which she had grown up in Philadelphia.
Prone to summer eczema, this dog had cost the
family what Angela's father described as a small
fortune. At the time it had been serious but not
overwhelming, as such a situation would be now.

All this flashed through Angela's mind in a split
second, while her mother stood looking at Chip's
shining face. It was going to be hard to disappoint
him—terribly hard!—but it had to be done, and from
some dark, unhappy recess of her mind Angela
dredged up the idea that there was even a sort of
justice in the denial. Because her own hopes had
been crushed, she actually welcomed the prospect
of a fellow sufferer. It would make her feel less
alone.

Crouching, Chip lowered the puppy gently to the
floor. "He *gave* him to me," he repeated softly.
"Isn't he beautiful?"

As he spoke, the setter gamboled and skidded
across the linoleum and Angela watched her mother

bend to receive the caress of a rough pink tongue.

"He is completely wonderful," Janet Dodge said, and took a long, decisive breath. "Have you named him yet?"

CHAPTER ⟨ *six*

"It's not fair!" Angela stormed. "It's not fair at all and you know it!" She was standing with her hands clenched, facing her mother across the living-room coffee table. Although she kept her voice lowered so that Chip should not be awakened, she intended to have this out.

"There are a number of things in life that are not fair, Angie." Janet Dodge spoke with careful restraint. "I wish you'd try to see this from my point of view. I wish you'd try to understand."

"Understand!" Angela sniffed disdainfully. "I understand all right. Who do you care about in this family? Chip!"

"Of course I care about Chip, just as I care about you." Leaning forward, Mrs. Dodge rested her elbows on her knees and clasped her hands so tightly that the knuckles showed white. "But I had

70

a choice to make tonight. Chip is nine years old,
Angie, with a child's fierce ardor. That puppy is as
necessary to him as breathing. I couldn't break his
heart."

Angela, unconsciously dramatic, beat her chest
with a fist. "What about me?"

"You're five years older than Chip. In some
countries girls your age are being married; in others
they are earning their own living. You are almost
grown-up."

Angela didn't feel grown-up. She felt wronged
and she felt frustrated, but she didn't feel grown-up
at all. "I don't care whether I'm nine or ninety,"
she insisted. "It's not fair!"

"Perhaps not. But the ski boots and the puppy
just aren't the same thing."

"Why aren't they?"

"The puppy is a living creature to which Chip is
able to give a great deal of pent-up love. The boots
are material things."

"But just as necessary to me as a dog is to him."

"Are you sure?"

"Of course I'm sure!" Angela turned and walked
up and down the room, seething. Then she came
over and pounded a fist on the coffee table. "I'm
going to get some boots that fit me," she said. "I'm
going to learn to ski if it's the last thing I ever do!"

"Bravo," said her mother, with a voice as cool as
her gray eyes, which had acquired a steely glint.

Angela, meeting them, knew that for the first time she was being faced by an adult and given no quarter. "Just be certain," Janet Dodge said, "that you are not pursuing a whim."

A whim. Angela remembered the word, because it cut her and because it recalled an expression she had once heard: "a whim of iron." Helping around the house over the week end, she went about her tasks with a sullen resentment. Only before the paying guests did she pretend to be affable, and this cost her an effort, because they kept talking to her about Chip's dog.

"Isn't he a darling?"

"Don't you just adore him, Angie?"

"Come here, boy! Look, he's learned to give me his paw."

Everyone suggested names for the pup, making a game of choosing something special, and Chip sat starry-eyed in their midst, considering and discarding, until somebody suggested "Christie" and he nodded his head.

"Christie. It's a skiing word, isn't it?" He looked to his sister for confirmation, but Angela took no notice.

"That's right," Mrs. Dodge agreed, "and this is a ski lodge. Very appropriate."

"Christie." Chip tried the name again. "Here, Christie!"

The pup came to him at once, tumbling over his

own long legs and landing in a heap in the boy's lap.

"See, he knows his name already," said one of the house guests. It seemed a happy choice.

But Angela stood apart from the conversation and was quick to find an errand in the kitchen, so that she wouldn't be expected to contribute her comment. The fact that the puppy was so very endearing, so anxious to please and so full of adoration for all human beings made her isolationist attitude difficult to maintain, but she persevered. The world was against her, and Angela was against the world, but even in the face of total war she laid her plans —and Monday she started to carry them out.

Skipping lunch at school, she took the Townsends' gift boots to a Manchester ski shop and asked what they'd be worth as a trade-in on another pair.

The owner of the store inspected them critically. "They're pretty beat-up," he said. "On a new pair I could allow you maybe . . . well, three dollars. That's all."

Angela swallowed. "I hadn't been thinking of a new pair," she admitted. "I was hoping I could make an exchange on something secondhand."

At once the proprietor lost interest. "That's not the way we trade," he said. "Old boots are just used for rentals." He dismissed the proposition with a shrug.

But Angela was persistent. She put her pride in

her pocket and explained the whole situation, even admitting that she had been trying to ski in jodphur boots. At this the man stared at her, then gave a low whistle. "Come on back to the storeroom," he invited her. "I'll see what I've got."

Sorting through a pile of ancient boots which had been ticketed with size numbers and then thrown, hit or miss, into a corner, he came up with a couple of pairs which Angela could try on. The first were too large, but the second, though far from a perfect fit, were wearable.

"These would do just fine!"

The man said, "O.K. We'll make a swap. Your old boots and five bucks."

Angela didn't stop to consider whether this was fair or not. "I—I don't have the money right now," she admitted, "but I can get it. Would you save them for me?"

"For Pete's sake, sister, have a heart! I go to all this trouble and *now* you tell me you don't have the dough." He picked up the boots and tossed them back on the pile. "I'm not in business for charity."

Desperation made Angela think fast. She pulled off the wrist watch her father had given her when she was graduated from grammar school and held it out. "You can have this for collateral."

Again the store owner stopped and looked at her curiously, as though he was trying to see inside the mind of this tall, slender girl with the intense brown eyes. Something made him put out his hand and take the watch from her, and Angela was aware for the first time in her life of a sense of personal power.

"Darnedest deal I ever made," the fellow muttered uncomfortably. "Here. You keep your watch. I'll trust you for the dough."

But Angela shook her head. "No," she said firmly. "The watch is worth about twenty-five dollars. And you see I'd like to charge some poles, too."

She carried her equipment home that afternoon, eleven dollars and ninety-five cents in debt and quite unable to imagine how she could ever tell her mother about the watch. But Daddy wouldn't have minded, she kept thinking. He would have understood. And I'll get the watch back somehow. I'll put up a notice in the post office and advertise for baby-sitting jobs.

As a matter of fact Mrs. Dodge, following the *laissez-faire* policy she had adopted the night before, made no comment at all about the watch, and Angela couldn't be sure that she even noticed its absence. About the boots and poles, which Angela explained cursorily as "a swap I made," she said very little; and the fact that she appeared neither to approve or disapprove made her daughter more uncomfortable than a downright scolding. She felt like a stranger in her own home.

But once out on the slope behind the house, in boots which the bindings of her skis could really

grab, holding poles which were light and manage-
able, nothing counted except a wonderful new feeling of freedom. Now at last she could have fun!

Right away, on her very first run, she acquired a
sense of power which was to grow with each day's
practice. Now she was in command of her skis;
they no longer went skittering off without her at
the slightest provocation. Now she could work on
the techniques to which Dave had introduced her.
And soon she would be ready to try an honest-to-
goodness slope!

A teachers' convention offered a providential
holiday in the middle of the following week, and
Angela seized the opportunity to spend the day at
Bromley. She had no money for the lifts, but she
had learned to climb and her leg muscles had grown
strong and accustomed to exercise which would
have tired many a seasoned skier. All day she practiced turns on the novice slope called the Lord's
Prayer; and in the afternoon, just as she was about
to leave, Dave showed up, quite alone, with his skis
and poles over his shoulder.

"Hi, Angie. How's it going?"

"Better, thanks."

"I see you've got some boots."

Angela nodded, smiling.

"Been up any of the lifts?"

She shook her head.

"Come on, I'll treat you to a ride on the Poma and

bring you down the East Meadow," Dave invited
her casually. "Got to see how my pupil's doing."

The fact that he sounded faintly patronizing
never occurred to Angela. Excitement made her
eyes sparkle, and her cheeks were red from exertion.
"I'm not sure I'll be good enough to suit you," she
murmured, "but I'd love to try it. Thanks a lot."

She could see at once that Dave enjoyed playing
the expert. He showed her how to handle the lift
and demonstrated his own ease. Then, at the top
of the slope, he suggested, "Let me go first. Then
try to follow me. I'll wait for you after a couple of
turns."

Angela nodded. "Remember, I'm still a beginner."

Grinning, Dave pushed off and called over his
shoulder, "A snow bunny, you mean."

But by the time they reached the red-painted
shelters at the bottom of the slope Angela could feel
that Dave's attitude had subtly changed. To her
own surprise she had been able to traverse and turn,
schuss and snowplow, in precise imitation of the
pace Dave set. He looked at her in astonishment
mingled with a certain unconcealable masculine
jealousy.

"Who's been coaching you?"

"Nobody. You know that."

"Come off it!"

"Honestly, Dave. I've been working out in the back pasture, up until today."

Angela was aware, because Dave's breath was coming in jerks and because hers was quite steady, that the discipline she had imposed upon herself was evident. The daily jog trot along the road which led from the highway to the farmhouse, the exhausting climbs—herringbone or side-step—up her practice slope, the setting-up exercises she forced herself to do every morning—all these things were paying off. Dave, though a far more experienced skier, was soft by comparison. She doubted, at this point, if he'd have the stamina to climb the Lord's Prayer even once.

"You're going to be O.K.," he muttered, as though the comment were forced from him against his will. "Of course you've got to learn to tuck your fanny in and keep your skis closer together and about a hundred million other things, but you're going to be all right."

It was manna from heaven to Angela. She looked at him as Chip looked at his setter, with eyes full of adoration. "Do you really think so?" she breathed. "Will you teach me everything you know?"

"Hey! Wait a minute. Why should I?" Dave's expression was half teasing, half puzzled, but as he stood watching her loosen the bindings and take off her skis, Angela glanced up with a sudden awareness. For the first time he was seeing her as a girl.

And instinctively she knew how to react. Lowering her lashes, she murmured, in a voice with just a suggestion of Ellen Whipple's purr, "You don't have to do a thing you don't want to, Dave, but I'd be awfully thrilled!"

CHAPTER $\begin{smallmatrix}\S\\\S\\\S\end{smallmatrix}$ *seven*

AT THIRTY-FIVE CENTS an hour, the current rate for baby-sitting in and around Peru, it would take quite a while to earn eleven dollars and ninety-five cents. But although the debt sometimes felt as heavy as an albatross hanging around her neck, at other times Angela could shake it off and forget all about it.

These were the times when she was on skis, the only hours in her life which really counted. At Burr and Burton she walked from class to class, from gym to lunchroom in a fog, neither knowing nor caring what the rest of her schoolmates were talking about or learning.

In the evening, whenever the notices she had posted in the General Store and Post Office brought a telephone call, she stayed with people's children. Although she took her schoolbooks along to these sitting jobs, she seldom opened them, procrastinating without any particular sense of guilt, dreaming her evenings away as she dreamed away the days, lost in a world of snow and skis, which was an escape from a reality she found too stern to face with her mother's fortitude.

The snow, which had come so late in the season, held through a long cold spell. New powder, so fluffy and dry that Angela could scoop it up like a handful of feathers, brought skiers to Vermont during early March, and again the Dodge farmhouse was full to overflowing with week-end guests.

Just before spring vacation Angela had a windfall. Mr. Henderson, for whom she had done a few extra services, waxing his new skis with loving care and making sure that he was handed a cup of piping hot coffee as soon as he appeared downstairs in the morning, presented her with a five-dollar bill.

At first Angela reacted instinctively. A tip? She felt like a servant. Drawing back, she almost said, "Oh, no."

But she bit the words back before they were spoken, and felt the crisp paper crush in the palm of her hand. "Thank you," she stammered, seesawing between reluctance and frank pleasure. "Thank you very much."

Mr. Henderson nodded and patted her briefly on the shoulder. "It'll take you up the lifts a few times," he said. "I've seen you out there doing it the hard way."

The lifts! Angela didn't tell him that she had ridden only once on the East Meadow tow and had never been on a lift in her life. She knew what she must do with the five dollars. She must add it to the four dollars and ninety cents she had already earned to clear off her self-imposed debt.

But Mr. Henderson's suggestion, once implanted, began to take root in her mind. Rationalizing, she told herself that this was a real bonanza, quite unconnected with the money she had acquired so laboriously to pay for her boots and poles. This she would squander—joyously, recklessly! This was a bequest of wings!

But although Angela's heart pounded with excitement, she said not one word to her mother about Mr. Henderson's gift. They existed, these days, in a state of unhappy truce, addressing one another without apparent feeling, living and working side by side without any sense of the companionship they once had shared.

Chip, occupied by his beloved setter, seemed unaware of the family rift. It seemed to Angela that his every waking thought was for Christie, who was growing visibly, week by week. The pup's appetite had become prodigious. He wolfed his meals and turned melting brown eyes to his master, begging for more.

But Chip was firm. He had promised his mother not to spoil the dog, and he held to the rules they

had worked out. No feeding between meals, no
racing through the house. Christie had learned to
come when called, to sit or lie down on command,
to stay on the place and not go wandering off, no
matter how tempting the smells that drifted down
from the birch woods behind the farm.

"A remarkable puppy," the paying guests called
him, and Chip nodded agreement, thinking privately that Christie was more than that. He was the
best ever, the most wonderful dog that had ever
been born. Angela could read her brother's
thoughts in his eyes, in his smile, in the special
glow which surrounded him. He looked plump
these days, as though he were so inflated with
happiness that he was about to burst.

But because of her quarrel with her mother,
Angela would not permit herself to accept Christie
on outwardly friendly terms. Only when she happened to find herself alone with the pup, when there
was no chance of detection, did she drop to the
floor to cuddle him, big and clumsy, in her arms,
and offer her cheek to the rough pink tongue which
caressed Chip's family and friends with impartial
and exuberant affection.

These moments were as rare as they were senti-
mental. Usually Angela held her feelings in check,
and concentrated on her one increasing purpose—to
get as much time as possible to ski.

Driving a businesslike bargain with her mother,

she arranged to work from eight until eleven every
morning of her spring holiday, then be free until
five in the afternoon. When she couldn't get a lift
to Bromley she trudged to the main road with her
skis over her shoulder and deliberately broke a strict
family injunction. She thumbed a ride on a passing
truck.

Once at the slopes, she was in seventh heaven.
Alternate freezing and thawing under the early
spring sun had formed a surface of distinct kernels
on the snow.

"Like tapioca pudding," Angela said to Dave,
when she met him waiting in line for one of the
lifts. "Good, isn't it?"

He nodded but corrected her. "The skiers call
this kind of snow 'pure corn.'"

Dave was skiing with another boy, whom he introduced as Ted Jameson, home from preparatory
school for the holidays. They chatted together
casually as they waited for their turns on the J-bar.
"Pupil of mine," Dave told Ted, bragging. "Wait
till you see her ski."

Angela preened in the warmth of the compliment,
although she realized that Dave's intent was not
entirely selfless. She came down the Shincracker
ahead of the boys, taking care with her turns, working on her style, keeping her skis neatly together
and parallel. It never once occurred to her to be
ashamed of the blue jeans which were tucked into

the tops of her heavy woolen socks, or to envy the
other girls who dotted the slopes with their bright
hoods and parkas. She felt relaxed and completely
happy in the moment. With her hair streaming
behind her ears, her eyes sparkling in spite of their
squint against the snow's brightness, and her cheeks
red with wind burn, this wasn't Angela Dodge who
came flying down the long white trail. It was her
alter ego, the girl she wanted to be.

The impression she created on Ted Jameson was
quite unexpected. He found her gay and carefree
and competent, and he liked what he found. "You
mean Dave Colby taught you to ski like that?" he
asked in frank admiration, when he caught up to
her at the bottom of the slope. "In one season?
You're almost as good as he is right now."

"Oh, no!" Angela replied, shocked. "I'm still just
a beginner. But I love it!"

I love it, I love it, her heart sang, and she smiled
at both boys without vanity. "I wish you'd explain
counterrotation to me. I hear people talking about
it and I don't know what they mean."

Dave and Ted looked at one another and laughed.
"You're doing it without knowing it," Dave told her,
and as they turned toward the lift once more the
three of them became absorbed in technical talk.
For Angela the boys were her mentors, her betters,
and she gave them her complete attention and allegiance. For them she was that rare and delightful

thing, a girl truly devoted to a sport. Time sped.
The sun sank behind the mountains, and Angela,
completely engrossed, forgot to watch Bromley's
big clock and arrived home at five-fifteen.

"I'm sorry," she apologized, struck by a belated
sense of guilt as she came through the door. She
sank down on a kitchen chair and started to unlace
her boots without looking at her mother, who was
measuring coffee into a percolator.

Janet Dodge didn't scold. She didn't even reply
for a minute. Then she said, "Get out of those wet
clothes as quickly as possible and set all three tables
in the dining room. We have some extras for dinner
tonight and I'm running late."

Angela winced inwardly at her mother's use of the
personal pronoun. Not *you* but *I*. She carried her
boots to the alcove behind the wood stove and
hurried upstairs to change, aware for the first time
that she was dog-tired and that she had three hours
of hard physical labor ahead.

But the next day she forgot her weariness and
thought only of getting out again to the slopes. The
sun was so bright that she feared this might be the
last of the skiing. As she started down the road she
noticed that the brook was running high and that a
drip-drip-drip of melting snow sounded a tattoo
against last autumn's leaves. Mrs. Nickerson, coming by in her station wagon, picked Angela up and
gave her a lift all the way to Bromley, where buses

and private cars were causing a traffic jam. As they edged along in the stream of cars Mrs. Nickerson shook her head at the confusion and the noise.

"They always remind me of two different flights of ducks," she told Angela, "one quacking about skiing all winter and the other about golf all summer. I don't know which strikes me funnier."

Angela smiled politely, but she felt sorry for Mrs. Nickerson, as she did for her own mother, and for all adults who didn't understand the thrill a person could get from a sport. She thanked her and left with a sense of release, once more on her own, with five hours of freedom stretching ahead.

The trampled area around the shelters was swarming with people, who looked like brightly colored beetles with slender metal poles for antennae and skis for wings. Ted Jameson emerged from the throng and waved to Angela, then disappeared in a group lined up at the base of the lift.

Angela inspected her wallet ruefully and followed. After lunch she'd be out of money and doing it the hard way again, but meanwhile she intended to have fun. Impatiently she waited for her turn on the J-bar, then settled back comfortably against the stick and let it carry her to the top.

It was so warm she didn't need the sweater she was wearing, so she pulled it off and tied it around her waist. Although she looked around for Ted she didn't see him. Not that it mattered, really. It was just as much fun to ski alone.

Coming down the West Meadow well under control, relishing the ease with which her skis skidded around to the traverse as she practiced her christies, Angela was suddenly aware of a novice swooping past her. That girl should never be on this slope, she thought, and in the same instant watched her take a spectacular head-first plunge downward, then roll like a thrashing egg beater and land with a thump against a tree.

She was the nearest person, so she changed her traverse and skied over. "You all right?"

The girl, who was still trying to untangle her skis and poles, was pale and obviously frightened. "My ankle!" she whimpered. "I've twisted it, I guess. I don't think I can stand up."

"Don't try," Angela advised. "Wait a minute. Give yourself a chance. That was quite a spill."

The girl nodded sheepishly. "I guess I should have stuck to the Lord's Prayer," she admitted. "It's pretty icy out here today."

At that moment Ted Jameson skied up. "Casualty?" he asked.

"I hope not," Angela told him. "See if you can get up now," she suggested to the white-lipped girl.

Moving around to position cost her an effort, and when she tried to put any weight on the ankle she sank back. "I can't," she admitted. "I'm afraid you'll have to get help."

"You stay here," Angela found herself saying to Ted. "I'll go." Whether it was a desire to show off or to try her own speed she couldn't be sure, but even as she spoke she turned her skis and started to schuss downhill.

In the next few seconds she began to gather momentum alarmingly, and Dave's warning leapt into her mind too late. Slow skiing, easy skiing, was comparatively safe on these mended skis, but to schuss the West Meadow was foolhardy. Any stone protruding from this thin frozen crust was a hazard. She tried to edge her skis into the bluish snow and go into a turn, but the ice was impervious. Faster and faster she raced downward, fighting now only for balance, praying that she wouldn't crash into another skier who might be coming across the hill on a traverse.

The root which caught Angela's left ski was strong and wicked. She never even saw it, but she heard the tearing, splintering sound of the hickory and gasped as a searing pain struck at her leg. The pain and the sense of crashing merged into one and became a whirlpool sucking her down, down and under.

It was ten minutes later when she regained consciousness, shivering although she was snugly bundled in blankets on the toboggan which was her snow-borne ambulance.

CHAPTER *eight*

THE PLASTER CAST was as white as the Easter lilies which stood on a broad window sill in the living room of the Dodge farmhouse. These were a gift from the paying guests, and Angela glanced at them ruefully, estimating their probable cost, then looked down at her useless leg, stuck out in front of her on the couch.

It was my own fault, she told herself for the twentieth time, but it didn't help matters. The damage was done. "A nice clean fracture," the surgeon at the Rutland hospital had assured her. "We'll rig you up with a walking iron and you can get back to school in a week."

School! What did school matter? "How long will I be in a cast?"

"Six weeks."

Six weeks. It seemed forever. Angela bit her lip

in vexation and tossed the magazine she had been
holding back on the coffee table. To think that the
girl she had been dashing down the West Meadow
to rescue should merely have had a sprain!

This bit of information came from Dave, who had
stopped to say hello and too-bad-but-I-told-you-so
when he delivered the milk on Good Friday afternoon. Angela, still in some pain, had suffered his
head shaking in silence. It didn't help to be reminded that she had acted like a baby, trying to run
before she learned to walk.

Above her head Angela could hear the click of
women's heels on the wide board floors, mingled
with the tramp of men's heavier feet. Suitcases
were being snapped shut, luggage moved to the
hall and parked at the top of the stairs. The last
of the Easter skiers were departing. The season was
ended. Until summer brought a few elderly vaca-
tionists and occasional transients motoring through
the Green Mountains, business at the Dodge farmhouse was at an end.

It would be a relief, thought Angela, all too
conscious of the three hectic days just past, to have
the house to themselves once more. Then she
wouldn't be ridden by a persistent feeling of guilt
every time she caught a glimpse of her mother
hurrying about the household chores with which—
had it not been for the accident—she could have
helped.

Friday, Saturday, Sunday. Three nights with the
house full to overflowing. Dinner to cook and serve,
dishes to clear away, pots and pans to wash, and
finally, when the last of the skiers had gone yawning
to bed, ash trays to empty, tables to dust, and the
kitchen floor to scrub. Chip tried his little best to
help, but Angela knew just how sorely her services
were missed. Instead of a partner in the family
enterprise, Mrs. Dodge had in her daughter another
guest to wait upon, another mouth to feed.

Even the trip home from the hospital had taken
up an appalling amount of time—valuable time
when there were beds to be made, cooking to be
done, rooms to be cleaned. Angela marveled at the
competence of her mother under stress. Once her
initial alarm was allayed by the reassurance of the
doctor, she went quietly about speeding up the
household machinery, taking all sorts of short cuts
which Angela recognized as necessary but expensive.

Bakery-made desserts and rolls. Unthinkable!
Yet under the circumstances there was no alterna-
tive. And the skiers, sympathetic to a man, pre-
tended not to notice that the cooking for which
Mrs. Dodge was becoming celebrated was replaced,
on this final week end, by a mélange dumped out
of cans.

Most astonishing of all was the way in which the
mistress of the house maintained a semblance of

equanimity. Angela knew her mother must be bone-tired, yet she talked and joked with the guests at the dinner table, making no apologies for the new regime, which necessitated self-service. Running a successful guesthouse, Angela once more realized, required more than a knack for management. Listening to the dining-room chatter from the comparative isolation of her couch, she was aware that her mother's social gift fused the assorted people under her roof into a sort of temporary family, contented with one another and at ease.

" 'By, Angie. Take care now!"

"Don't try running down the lane."

"Better get the boys at school to autograph that cast. It looks mighty bare, child."

One by one, the departing guests stopped in the doorway for a teasing or serious farewell, and minutes later Angela could hear her mother calling good-by as a motor started or a horn tooted outside.

At last the house was quiet. They were gone. Gone to take up the lives they had left in Albany, in Boston, in New York. It always seemed odd to Angela that she knew nothing about these lives, really. Just that one of the men was a psychiatrist, another a writer, that one couple ran a sporting-goods business, and that another pair dealt in real estate. In Vermont, however, they were simply skiers, some expert, some mediocre, others just learning, still at the stage of making repeated sitz-

marks in the snow. Now that the season was over
she wondered if they would grieve—if they would
count the months, as she had already done—until
November, when once again they might read the
weather reports and hope for a white Thanksgiving
in the hills.

Coming into the room with the accumulated mail
of several days in her hands, Mrs. Dodge sank into
her rocker with a sigh. "I've looked at this every
time I've passed the desk," she admitted, "but I
haven't had a chance to open an envelope."

"Want me to slit them for you?" Angela offered.

"There aren't that many, thanks." Mrs. Dodge
kicked off her shoes and edged around so that she
could rest her feet on the fender. The fire was dy-
ing, but there was still warmth in the coals.

Angela plumped up the pillows behind her back
and squirmed a little, wishing Chip would come in
with Christie so that she wouldn't have to be with
her mother alone.

It was a strange fear, like the anticipation of a
scolding which hadn't come. Even on the trip from
the hospital in the station wagon, with Mrs. Dodge
driving against time, yet taking care to guard
Angela from any unnecessary bumps, nothing but
words of sympathy had been spoken. There was no
sign that her mother was impatient or aggrieved.

Yet in Angela's mind the estrangement born on
the night of Christie's appearance had grown with

every passing week. Although her mother and she still spoke casually to one another she was aware of a superficiality in their relationship, produced by disappointment in one and resentment in the other. Although they remained mother and daughter, they had ceased to be friends.

Brooding on this, Angela was scarcely aware that her mother had risen and was standing in front of the couch, holding out the easily recognizable Burr and Burton report form. She reached out and took it automatically, frowning as she did so. Now what?

The answer was only too obvious. As her eyes raced down the column of grades she was aware at once that she had failed in two subjects—math and science. Her frown deepened. What did it matter, anyway? She hated school!

"I think you owe me some explanation," Mrs. Dodge was saying wearily.

Angela shrugged. "Flunk now and avoid the June rush," she quipped with false bravado. Keeping her head bent was an easy way to avoid her mother's eyes.

"Angela!"

"Well, what do you want me to do? Burst into tears?"

"I think," said Mrs. Dodge very slowly, "that it would be more understandable."

Readying for attack, Angela stiffened. The forward thrust of her chin looked belligerent, but her

Fifteen

CHAPTER { *one*

IT WAS AUTUMN in Vermont, a quiet, Indian summer day without wind. Fallen leaves lay on the roof of the Dodge farmhouse like golden coins; and Angela, astonishingly, felt at peace with the world.

She walked up the mountain to the beaver dam and sat down in the sun by the side of the winding dirt road, leaning her head on her knees and feeling glad that it was Saturday. She liked being alone, welcomed and treasured the opportunity because it was so rare. A gift, really.

A birthday gift! Angela, fifteen today, had shaken her head when her mother asked, "Would you like to invite some of your friends for dinner?"

"I'd rather have a day completely to myself, with no responsibilities."

Actually what she wanted was just this—time to sit in the sun, time in which to dream, to take stock, to look ahead. Life had been going by at a gallop all summer, and for this one day she wanted to slow it down to a walk.

Since the unhappy Easter Sunday when she had threatened to run away from home, a great deal of water had flowed over this beaver dam, and several very important things had happened to Angela. She now looked back on the episode as the low point in her life, when everything and everybody seemed to be against her, but when actually she had needed just such a jolt to make her stop and think.

It was astonishing how clearly she could still remember the long weeks in the unwieldy plaster cast. Very gradually, as day followed monotonous day, and the weight of enforced inactivity began to turn her thoughts inward, she became convinced that her mother was not to be placated, that she meant what she so distinctly had said.

A straight B average or no more skiing.

It was an ultimatum, and as Angela slowly came to her senses she realized that she was faced with the biggest job she had ever tackled—a job that might even be impossible.

The books she had avoided all winter looked monumental in size, and when she opened one in the middle the text was so unfamiliar it might have been written in a foreign language. She didn't have the faintest glimmer of what the writer was talking about. All the days of dreaming were gone with the winter snows. How could she ever catch up?

Then, in a school assembly, the headmaster of Burr and Burton happened to quote the slogan of the U. S. Army Air Force. " 'The difficult we do immediately. The impossible takes a little longer.' " Angela kept repeating it over and over to herself, until it began to wave in her mind like a flag behind which she could march.

With this standard she went into battle. She propitiated her math and science teachers, enlisted their help, and got down to work. With the perseverence which was her best quality she tackled her studies as she had tackled skiing, wholeheartedly. The fact that her leg was broken actually helped, because it kept her from straying to a more attractive occupation. She was attentive and quick in class, and gradually her grades improved, until she had pulled up her second-term average in both questionable subjects.

Mrs. Dodge didn't embarrass her daughter with exceptional praise, but she told her in a dozen unspoken ways that she was pleased. Once more Angela and her mother began to live together with their former rapport. Once more they were a team of two, working side by side and enjoying their companionship.

Then, in late June, the Hendersons bought a house half a mile down the road for a summer place, and moved in with their family of four active children while painters and carpenters and plumbers came and went.

After the first week Mrs. Henderson phoned Angela. "Could you possibly take over with this brood of ours?" she asked in a rather frantic voice. "They keep ducking under stepladders and losing tools and getting smeared up with paint and—well, *you* know!"

Angela did not know, but she could imagine, because the age range of the young Hendersons, Peter, Paula, Ginger, and Mousie—a deceptive nickname! —was from nine to three. They were firebrands, all of them, with their father's enthusiasm, and they treated the newly acquired house like a permanent picnic ground.

"I thought you might take them off on expeditions, swimming, and so forth," Mrs. Henderson was saying. "Anything to keep them out of the way."

"You mean every day?"

"Well, every day it's clear."

They agreed on terms, at which Angela's heart leapt. This was baby-watching in a big way, and she envisioned not the money that would be hers by the end of the summer, but the new skis the money would buy. "I'll have to speak to Mother first," she remembered to say.

Mrs. Dodge, who was out in the truck patch running the cultivator between rows of string beans

and broccoli, offered no objection, although Angela
was aware that her help with the garden and with
the endless canning, preserving, jelly making and
freezing that went on during July and August,
would be missed. She tried to make up for her
absence by working early in the morning and during the evenings, extended by daylight-saving time.
And by the end of the first fortnight she was ready
to confess, "I'd rather be a farm laborer than a
nursemaid any day!"

The four young Hendersons were a handful.
Angela did her best to amuse and interest them.
She took them hiking. She taught them the habits
of the beavers and showed them how they had built
their great curved dam and their two-roomed lodge
out of boughs and mud and logs. She acted as a
lifeguard when they all went swimming at Hapgood's Pond, with even little Mousie thrashing about
in the icy water, quite beyond her depth.

"No, Mousie, you can't let Peter swim you to the
raft."

"I can, too."

"Not while I'm in charge. I'll tell you why. . . ."

Angela found herself dreading and hating the
endless disciplinary problems, but through them she
learned to discipline herself.

By the end of August the wallet in the top drawer
of her bureau was bulging with an accumulation of
bills. Fifty-eight hard-earned, magnificently useful

dollars. Skis! Ski pants and long red underwear such as real skiers wear. Boots that really fit!

Counting the money, Angela knew she couldn't have all these things and enough left over for a season ticket on the Bromley lifts, but it was fun to contemplate the prospect of making a choice, of deciding between this or that. Unless—a pin pricked the bubble with a painful jab—unless it was up to her to offer some of her earnings to her mother.

"I don't see why!" she said aloud, but her conscience contradicted her. The summer had been cold for Vermont, with long rainy spells, and only a very few tourists had found their way to the farmhouse door. The vegetable garden provided food, the apple and pear trees fruit, but more often than not there was no meat on the Dodges' dinner table. Angela knew quite well that it would be difficult to get along until the beginning of the winter season.

For several days she procrastinated. Then at last she went to her mother. "I have fifty-eight dollars," she said bluntly. "Do you need it?"

Janet looked up from one of Chip's socks which she was mending. "Of course I need it. *We* need it, I should say. But you earned it, Angie. This money is yours."

Angela gulped. "We could split it, maybe."

Her mother considered. "No. You do with it as you like."

"It was earned on your time, actually," Angela found herself saying. And to her own surprise and acute dismay she added, "I'd like to give half of it to you."

So now she had twenty-nine dollars in the top bureau drawer, twenty-nine dollars from the previous summer, plus a bit extra she had earned baby-sitting since school started. Lying back in the dry grass, looking up at the bright October sky, she considered it pensively. Enough, still, to buy secondhand skis and a season ticket on the lifts. The boots she had acquired last year would have to do.

A breeze stirred the branches of a tamarack tree, and a few inch-long needles drifted down like gentle rain, settling on Angela's plaid shirt and blue jeans. She stretched her legs and lifted her arms, yawning happily. What a lovely day!

Lovely, in spite of the warmth, because the falling tamarack needles were a promise that winter was on the way. Lovely because Angela no longer felt at war with her world, because being fifteen was going to be infinitely better than being fourteen, as she could already see.

Fall was a time for making plans, for plotting one's life, she decided. This year she would work hard in school, to please her mother, and she would learn to ski faultlessly, so that never again could she be deluded by the overconfidence which had caused her accident.

There was a plop in the water and she sat up very quietly, so that she would not disturb the beaver which had just come down a trail cut through the thicket on the far side of the pond. She could see the ripple he made in the water as he swam, with his flat tail acting as a rudder, and wondered what had taken him away from his lodge during the day, because she knew that the beaver family usually worked at night.

It had been Chip's chief sport, this summer, to walk up to the dam and watch the eager little builders at work. On dark nights he took along a flashlight, but when the moon was full this wasn't necessary, and he would sit by the hour watching the beavers cut down a tree, chip by chip, with their chisel-shaped teeth. Once, when they were alternately dragging and floating some timber to a spot where they were strengthening their dam, Angela had accompanied him, and on that evening she had developed an admiration for the busy creatures which brought her here again and again.

Christie was never allowed to come along, for fear the big pup would leap right into the pond in an attempt to make friends with the beaver family. Chip had trained the setter to stay on the place, teaching him the boundaries with great patience.

"If we were home I could take him to obedience school," he explained carefully to Angela. "But up here I've got to teach him myself."

It was increasingly rare, now, for Chip to refer to Philadelphia as home. He had eased himself into the Vermont way of life more completely than his sister, though if anyone had asked Angela, "Would you like to move back?" she would have shaken her head. Give up skiing? It was unthinkable.

It didn't occur to her that the reason might be more complex, and that she as well as Chip was beginning to love the farm. No one had ever told her that you inevitably feel close to the earth in which you work, that planting and weeding and grass cutting and apple picking each contributed to her sense of affection for the land they owned. She did know that she liked to touch the bark of the straight white birch in the woods beyond the meadow and know that these trees were theirs. She liked to fish for trout in the brook which tumbled downhill and bring three or four in for dinner. These things made her feel satisfied and good, just as sitting here beside the beaver dam did. They were Vermont things, totally unconnected with Philadelphia, and for this she was thankful, because she still missed her friends.

Not that she wasn't making friends in Peru, Angela thought as she got to her feet and started to scuff slowly along the road back to the farm. Well, perhaps not friends exactly, but good acquaintances. There was Dave, for instance, and Ted Jameson, who had started out as a skiing pal but

had showed up at Hapgood's Pond several times
this summer when he knew she'd be on hand with
her four small fry. Ted couldn't be considered a
beau. He was currently enamored of a girl in Bennington, concerning whom he talked to Angela at
length, but he was a nice boy and easy to be with.
She liked him.

She had also grown to like Barbara Benton, a girl
in her class at school who lived on the other side of
Styles Mountain. Barbara had been born in Vermont and she didn't chatter, but when she had
something to say it was usually interesting. She had
direct eyes, green flecked with brown like a bird's
egg, short-cropped reddish hair, a rangy, boyish
figure, and a passion for horses which matched
Angela's passion for skiing.

Frequently during the summer they had met on
the road, while Barbara was exercising her mare and
Angela was on her way to or from the Hendersons'.
At first they exchanged only a few words, but
gradually they fell into the habit of stopping to
talk, and by the time school opened they were on
very good terms, so that Angela felt less alone than
formerly.

Only one thing dismayed her about Barbara.
When she tried to interest her in skiing she seemed
almost as apathetic as Ellen Whipple. "But you're
missing so much!" Angela tried to tell her. "Here
you are, living right in a place people pay lots of

money to come to, and you don't take advantage of your opportunities."

Barbara had smiled. "I'm not the sort of person who can spread herself too thin," she explained. "You like skiing. I like horses. Why don't we let it go at that?"

Angela glanced up from the crisp bright leaves she was kicking before her as she walked along, half expecting to hear the clip-clop of horses' hoofs, because she was thinking about Barbara, but the road was empty as far as she could see ahead. A stone wall traced its way along the hillside at her right, crumbling in spots. It belonged to a burned-out farm, where only a couple of ancient lilac trees remained as a living memorial. Ground pine crept along the base of the wall, making Angela think of Christmas, and bright red checkerberry looked like holly peeping through the leaves.

As she came within sight of the house she could see her mother, down by the Rural Delivery box, standing with the day's mail tucked under one arm. She was reading a letter, and as Angela approached she glanced up.

"Hi, dear. Here's something very interesting."

"A check for a thousand dollars?"

Mrs. Dodge grinned. "Don't be so materialistic! It's a letter from the Bromley people asking if we'd like to take a young Swiss ski instructor to board."

"A Swiss ski instructor," breathed Angela reverently. "He's coming to Bromley?"

"So I understand."

Angela clasped her hands. "Oh, Mother, that's simply wonderful! We can, can't we—take him to board, I mean?"

Mrs. Dodge weighed the question. "It would mean giving up one of our rooms. It would mean we'd have to turn down some of the week-end ski trade we've built up so laboriously."

"But to have him living right under our roof," Angela said softly, "to be able to ask him questions and know you were getting the right answers. Why, he might even give me free lessons! Please, Mother. Let's!"

CHAPTER *two*

JACQUES BRUNNER was due to arrive at the Dodge
farmhouse on Sunday, November 18, and on Saturday Angela turned out the room he was to occupy,
with the vigor of a devoted lackey preparing a
bedchamber for a king.

Christie came and stood in the doorway, looking
puzzled. What's all this fuss about, his limpid dark
eyes seemed to say.

"We're going to have a man in the house," Angela
told him. "A guy who's been practically raised on
skis. If you don't think that's exciting, *I do*."

She got the short stepladder and washed the
closet shelves with ammonia and water. The Swiss
were very clean people, she had heard, and she
didn't want an American home to seem less than
immaculate to this stranger on their shores.

She cut new paper linings for the bureau drawers

and dusted the back of the mirror, to her mother's amusement. "I don't think he's going to be *that* meticulous," she said.

"You never know," Angela replied, without annoyance. "We want to make a good impression. If we don't, he may move somewhere else."

"There's a bare possibility," suggested Janet Dodge, "that we may *want* him to move somewhere else."

Angela whirled around, shocked. "Why?"

"Well, we don't know very much about this fellow, actually. He's a foreigner, and he's accustomed to an entirely different sort of atmosphere. He may not fit in."

"He speaks English, doesn't he?"

"Yes," Mrs. Dodge admitted. "Fluently, I understand. I guess otherwise he couldn't teach skiing to Americans."

Angela helped her mother turn the mattress on the antique cherry four-poster and went to bring fresh sheets from the linen closet. "Do you know how old he is?"

"Twentyish, I understand."

"That's not so old," said Angela, from her new estate of fifteen. "There's a girl in my class at school who has dates with a man of twenty."

"Ridiculous," murmured Mrs. Dodge.

"It's true, though."

"Well, don't let it give you any ideas. When you

start having dates, it will be with boys your own age, or close to it, like Dave or Ted."

Angela hid her blush by turning to stuff a pillow into a slip. It was embarrassing, at her age, to have had no actual dates with anyone. She cast a quick glance in the mirror as she returned the pillow to the bed, and was depressed by what she saw, a thin, lightly freckled face with great dark eyes and a mouth that didn't seem made for lipstick. Her hair was wrong too. It kept getting in her way, so she had caught it back with a big barrette which made her look childish. I'll do something about myself, she promised her reflection. I'll try out some of the hair-dos they show in magazines. Maybe I'll even pluck my eyebrows!

"We don't even know that Jacques Brunner isn't married," Mrs. Dodge remarked.

"Married? He can't be!"

"It's perfectly possible. Europeans frequently marry young."

"I don't believe he's married," Angela murmured, half to herself, but some of her sense of anticipation disappeared.

As a matter of fact, it was just as well, because when Jacques arrived he wasn't at all what she expected. And what had she expected, really? A modernized knight-on-a-white-charger? A life-sized reproduction of a Swiss travel poster instructor, complete with parka and red knitted cap?

Mr. Brunner, as Angela called him at first, was a slender, shaggy-haired young man in rumpled clothes, distinguishable from the other passengers who dismounted from the New York bus in Manchester Depot only by the deep tan of his skin, sunburned winter and summer until it had a weathered, permanent color which was quite different from the pasty look of the city dwellers with whom he was traveling.

Angela's mother went forward, easily cordial, and introduced herself and her children. "You had a pleasant trip?"

"Very pleasant," replied the young man with a French accent. He smiled and Angela noticed that although his teeth were white and even, unfortunately one had been filled with gold.

Chip insisted on lugging the larger of Mr. Brunner's suitcases, although it was too heavy for him, and he grunted as he heaved it into the back of the station wagon. Angela, awkward because she was disillusioned, stood and looked on while the bus driver pulled a pair of skis from the luggage compartment and the Swiss carried them over and angled them gently into the wagon so that they rested against the rear seat.

"Why, they're an American make!" she commented in surprise.

Jacques nodded. "We like the Head skis in Switzerland," he told her. "They are expensive, but

most of the instructors buy them, because they are
good for all-round purposes. For racing, however,
some people prefer hickories."

"Why?" asked Angela as they got into the car,
she and Chip riding in the back seat and their new
boarder in front with Mrs. Dodge.

"You are a skier?" Jacques asked with some
interest before he replied.

"I am learning."

"Then you may understand what I mean when I
tell you that these skis chatter—and sometimes
wander—at speeds over fifty miles an hour."

"Fifty miles an hour!" Chip said in astonishment.
"Can *you* go that fast?"

Jacques Brunner, turning in the seat to look back
at the child, smiled and nodded. "Perhaps faster,"
he confessed.

Mrs. Dodge laughed. "Be careful, Mr. Brunner.
You will become a hero even before we have
reached Peru."

The young man smiled and changed the subject.
"Peru. It is an odd name for a village, I think."

"It came about in a strange way. A long time ago
a vein of gold was found in the mountains. It soon
petered out, but the rumor of its existence brought
a flock of prospectors. It was during this local gold
rush that somebody dreamed up the name of Peru."

"Like Peru in South America," Chip felt called
upon to explain.

"How very interesting," Jacques murmured. But his attention had been diverted by a ski shop which they were passing. Then came the familiar inns, strung along Route 11: the Red Doors, Johnny Seesaw's, Wiley's. Mrs. Dodge pointed them out and explained that each one was booked to capacity during the holiday season—if (the inevitable *if*) there was snow.

"But no large hotels?" asked Jacques in some surprise. "Or are they elsewhere? In Villars, where I come from, there are several hotels." He started to enumerate them. "The Palace, the Hotel du Parc, the Marie Louise—"

"Not here," Janet Dodge explained. "Here it is different. People stay at inns or in guesthouses or ski lodges. There would be no business for a big hotel in the summertime."

Bromley, when they came to it, looked very bright, the red buildings standing out with Christmas-card vividness against fresh snow which had fallen the night before. He couldn't be seeing it at a better time, Angela thought, excitement surging within her as it always did when she looked at the slopes. Mrs. Dodge slowed down and pulled up beside the road. "Here is where you will work, Mr. Brunner," she said.

Jacques said nothing for a few seconds; and Angela, watching him, saw a flicker of disappointment cross his face. "It will be different," he remarked finally, "from the Alpine slopes to which I am accustomed. There are so many trees!"

"But the trails are very good," Angela said, instantly on the defensive.

"I am sure they are," replied Jacques politely.

"There are four lifts and three rope tows."

"Oh?"

"And the East Meadow is an open slope. It's supposed to be like Switzerland."

Jacques nodded and smiled with such an obvious effort that Angela realized that he was homesick. Suddenly the gold tooth didn't matter. Her heart went out to him, because he looked so unexpectedly forlorn.

She tried to think of something kind to say, something distracting. "Your English is very good, Mr. Brunner." But the words sounded stiff and formal. They didn't accomplish their purpose. The young man said, "Thank you very much," as though he had scarcely heard her, and Mrs. Dodge pulled out into the highway and drove on.

After a rather strained silence it was Chip who saved the day. "Do they have any wild animals where you live?" he asked their guest.

Jacques said, "A few. Fox, of course, and chamois."

"What's a shamwah?"

"A sort of mountain goat. You have them here, no?"

"No," Chip replied. "We have lots of deer, though. You can see their tracks, any old time, coming right down to the back steps."

"Do you have ermine?" Jacques asked.

"Is that a weasel?" Chip wanted to know.

Jacques nodded. "A brown weasel that turns white in the winter."

"Do we, Mother?"

"I've never seen one, but I suppose we do."

"We have bears!" announced Chip proudly. "Big brown bears. They'll squeeze you to death if they catch you, so you'd better watch out."

"Chip!" Angela remonstrated. "He's teasing, Mr. Brunner."

The young man began to smile again. "In America I understand everyone uses the first name. Please, will you call me Jacques?"

After that everything seemed to become easier. Christie, who was introduced proudly by Chip, bounded around the house to greet them as they drove in and made a tremendous fuss over the newcomer. Angela carried the skis to the back porch while Jacques and her brother went ahead with the bags. The house looked warm and welcoming, and she knew that their new boarder was impressed by it. The antiques which she had scorned—the lowboy and the corner cupboard, the walnut dining room table with slender Hepplewhite legs, and all the others looked mellow and rich and full of atmosphere. For the first time she was glad to own them, and aware that her mother's sure taste made their setting special and individual. She was proud of her home.

The room assigned to Jacques delighted him. He liked the bright quilted coverlet on the bed and the deep window seat and the bookcases. "I know what I shall do in the evenings," he said when he came downstairs after unpacking. "I shall read and improve my English. That will be very good."

"You don't need to improve your English," said Chip in a man-to-man fashion. "It's O.K. as it is. Why don't you teach me French instead?"

"Chip!" Angela remonstrated again, but Jacques didn't seem to mind. "I'll make a bargain. Will you learn ten French words a day?"

"It sounds like an awful lot," Chip murmured, retreating.

"All right then," his mother said. "The deal's off."

Jacques looked confused. "The deal's off?" he repeated.

"That's slang," Angela told him, and explained.

The boy and the young man argued the question back and forth, half teasing, half serious. By dinner-time they were on a casually friendly basis; and Angela, helping her mother in the kitchen, whispered, "He's not exactly pretty, but he's sort of nice, isn't he?"

Mrs. Dodge nodded. "I think Bromley was a bit of a shock. To a Swiss it must look small."

"Small?" Such a thing had never occurred to Angela, but in the next few days, as she came to know Jacques better, she began to understand what her mother meant.

He talked to her about his family's chalet, and about the ski resort of *Villars-sur-Ollon,* where he had been born.

"Why *sur-Ollon?*" Angela wanted to know.

"Because there are many villages named Villars in Switzerland. Thirty, perhaps. This is to distinguish it from the others. That is all."

"Vee-lar," repeated Angela. "The way you pronounce it is pretty. What is the town like?"

Jacques told her how the single shopping street edged in against the side of the mountain, and how the great luxury hotel named the Palace hung high above the station, to which a gayly painted little train climbed hourly from Bex, a town on the floor of the Rhone valley, ten miles below. He showed her picture post cards of the carved wooden chalets which dotted the mountainside above the village.

"They look like doll's houses," Angela said.

"They are very carefully made, and very warm. Every night the shutters are closed, so that the whole village seems to go to sleep."

"Tell me more about the skiing," Angela begged.

"There are classes for beginners on the golf

course," Jacques replied patiently. "Then at the hotels there are lifts. But the really good skiers take the funicular up to Bretaye, a thousand feet higher. Here the snow comes early, even in September, and lasts a long time."

"And Bretaye is more open than Bromley."

"Oh, yes." Jacques sounded surprised. "A great deal of it is above the tree line, you see. From the top of any one of the mountains you can see for many kilometers. It is like standing at the top of the world."

Angela was insatiable. She wanted to know about every lift, every tow. She plied Jacques with all sorts of questions. When had he first started to ski? How fast was it possible for a person to improve each season?

"You are speaking of yourself?"

"Yes," Angela admitted, ducking her head.

"I would have to see you ski first."

"The trouble is, I don't get much chance. After school it's too late—too dark."

Jacques nodded sympathetically. "In Villars we arrange it better. The school children ski in the early afternoon, then return for tea and classes which last until seven."

"I wish they'd do that here," Angela breathed enviously.

"What about Saturday?" Jacques suggested. "I must teach a class, it seems, at ten o'clock in the

morning, but after that I am free for an hour if no
one requires a private lesson. Of course," he
warned, "of that I can not be sure."

Angela's sigh trembled. "I'll try," she promised.
"If Mother doesn't need me—"

"Of that, too, you can never be sure?"

She nodded, warmed by his understanding.

"There is no hurry. We have the entire winter
ahead."

"But it goes so fast. So very fast! And then—for
weeks, sometimes—there is no snow."

"Do not say that," Jacques warned. "Do not even
think it. This season will be better. It must be. I
shall earn a great deal of money in order to send
for—how do you say it?—for my sweetheart? She
would like to come to the United States too."

Angela's eyes grew interested. "Are you engaged,
then—engaged to be married?" She felt as though
they were talking on a very adult level, as though
Jacques had taken her into his confidence, as indeed
he had.

The young man nodded proudly and took a wallet
out of his pocket. "You would like to see her picture?"

"Yes, please."

He handed her a snapshot of a plump, smiling
girl wearing a raincoat and a bandanna. "She is
pretty, no?"

"Very pretty," Angela said. "Can she ski well?"

Jacques shrugged. "She can ski, but she does not care about it as you do. She wishes to marry and have children, that is all."

CHAPTER three

ON SATURDAY MORNING Angela dashed through her household chores with headlong speed, and her mother, who was going to market in Manchester, dropped her off at Bromley just before ten-thirty.

She was carrying her new skis—secondhand, actually, but new to her!—and she was wearing a pair of ski pants which Mrs. Henderson had discarded and which Angela had managed to nip in with safety pins around the too-ample waist. They were a great improvement over blue jeans.

But most important was the money she carried in her pocket—money for a season ticket on the lifts. No longer would she have to waste valuable hours plodding back up the slopes down which she could ski in a matter of minutes. In exchange for the money, she soon held in her hand a piece of cardboard which was like a passport to a new world—a

white world of snow and speed and excitement.
Now the long hours of struggling with the will-
fulness of the Henderson foursome seemed worth
every minute. In exchange she had been able to
buy adventure, and nothing else mattered. This
winter she would no longer be a snow bunny. This
winter she would really be able to ski!

Jacques, finished with his class, came gliding over
to meet her. "I do have a private lesson," he told
her matter-of-factly, "but I'll take a bit off my lunch
hour if you want to meet me here at twelve."

"I hate to ask you to do that."

"It's all right. With the big American breakfast a
midday meal is not very important."

Angela was ready and waiting when the hands of
the big clock reached five minutes to twelve. Her
muscles were warmed up from a couple of runs and
she felt relaxed and resilient. To play safe because
of her broken leg, she had been doing special exercises since fall, and she knew she was in excellent
physical condition.

Jacques shook hands with his private pupil, a
pink and breathless middle-aged woman, just a
minute or two after the hour had struck, and skated
over to Angela nonchalantly. "Let's try the Boulevard," he suggested. "I want to see you make some
turns."

Skiing ahead, he told her to wait a minute, then

follow his lead; and after each turn he leaned on
his poles and watched her critically.

The first thing he said surprised Angela. "You
must learn how to breathe properly."

"Breathe?"

"Yes. On the snow you must bring breathing into
accord with your movements. You must exhale
more air than you breathe in, so that you expel all
the carbon dioxide. Remember this fundamental—
short inhalation and long, deep exhalation in rhythm
with what you are doing. It will help. Try it. You
will see."

Angela meant to try, but she found herself more
concerned with the swiveling action of her feet and
the smoothness of her turns this morning. Jacques
waited for her at the bottom of the slope and
nodded his head. "You have ease and a sense of
sureness. You will make a fine skier, some day, if
you will practice and acquire technique."

"I will do anything!" Angela assured him. "Anything!" Her face was aglow with anticipation. "A
fine skier." It was a promise. And "some day"
seemed very near at hand.

She practiced alone until one-thirty, then caught
a bus back to Peru and walked from the village to
the farm rapidly, in spite of the heavy skis balanced
on one shoulder. On the way she concentrated on
the breathing Jacques considered so important.
Inhale for two steps, exhale for six. At first it seemed

unnatural and difficult, but gradually she became accustomed to the exercise and realized that her instructor was right. She felt less fatigued than when she breathed normally in the cold.

Later, in the kitchen, she hummed a happy little tune as she peeled potatoes for dinner. And that evening when she served the skiing guests and listened to their conversation with Jacques, she felt privileged to be on the outskirts of the group, even though she was not a part of it. Every bit of skiing talk was to be sifted and stored away in her memory for the time when she might need it, later on.

Of course, Angela realized, not a single one of the week-end guests realized that they had a potentially fine skier in their midst. It was a secret she shared with Jacques alone, a secret she hugged to herself as strenuously as Chip was right now hugging his beloved Christie, on the hearthrug before the living-room fire. It was a secret she could afford to keep, because it wouldn't be a secret forever. Ahead of her loomed that glorious "some day" when Jacques' promise would come true.

For the Thanksgiving week end, unofficial opening of the winter season, Mrs. Dodge hired extra help from the village, a girl by the name of Esther Byley, who was a class ahead of Angela in school.

Esther was a large, rather cowlike girl with an oily skin and straight pale brown hair which she had permanently waved with a home-beauty kit.

She worked with apparent slowness but so methodically that she actually accomplished more than Angela, and her favorite topic of conversation was boys.

"The reason I'm working is to earn money for a new 'formal,' " she felt called upon to explain. "Then if I get a date for the Christmas dance I'll be all set."

"Aren't you sort of putting the cart before the horse?"

Esther looked blank.

"I mean—shouldn't you get the date before the dress?"

"Not necessarily," Esther said, patting her hair, which she could see reflected in the kitchen window. "I believe in being prepared."

Angela looked increasingly doubtful. She couldn't imagine what kind of boy would like to steer Esther around a dance floor. Certainly nobody like Dave.

Yet whenever Dave's jeep bounced into the lane, the Dodges' new helper seemed to find urgent business on the back porch. "She almost moos when she sees him," Angela whispered to her mother angrily. "I never saw such an exhibition in my life."

"Sh!"

"I don't care. I think it's disgusting!"

"Jealous, dear?"

The idea had never occurred to Angela, but while

she denied it hotly she privately pondered the question. Was she annoyed at Esther because she missed the moments when, on delivering the milk, Dave had stopped to chat with her?

The next Monday, passing him in the hall, she glanced at him warily, mumbled a brief hello, and would have walked on, but he grabbed her arm. "Are you avoiding me, or what?"

"Avoiding you? Why should I avoid you?"

Dave shrugged. "How do I know? But you didn't give me a tumble when I passed you on the Shincracker yesterday."

"I didn't see you," Angela said honestly.

"You don't seem to see anybody these days, except that Swiss pro."

"Oh, Dave, that's not true!" Angela was genuinely shocked. "I've been working with him, yes—every time he can give me a few spare minutes. He's teaching me a lot, Dave. He's wonderful!"

Dave's eyebrows drew together. "I thought you thought so."

Angela moved over toward the wall, so that other students could pass. "You know what I mean. A wonderful instructor. He's older, Dave. He's twenty. And he's got a girl back home. He's engaged to be married," she said in a rush. "I've seen her picture. Her name's Marie."

Still frowning, Dave snapped back at her, "Then why doesn't he stop cradle snatching over here?"

Thoroughly annoyed now, Angela stamped her foot. "Don't be silly. It isn't like that, and you know it!" Then, remembering all Dave's help last year, she suggested placatingly, "Meet me at Bromley this Sunday and I'll show you a few of the things I've been learning. You'll be interested."

Still looking far from mollified, Dave said, "Oh, so now you're going to show me! That *is* a switch!"

Angela stood quite still, biting her lip. Every time she opened her mouth she seemed to put her foot in it. Was there nothing she could say that would be right?

Finally her very silence, along with the concern shining so steadily in her dark eyes, turned the trick. "Forget it," Dave muttered, patting her shoulder gruffly. "I'm just in a bad humor, I guess."

The next day he passed a note all the way across study hall to tell her that he'd like to meet her on Sunday. "Noon at the Wild Boar?" it said. "Or shall I pick you up at your house?"

Angela wrote back: "I would love it if you'd come for me. Otherwise I'll have to walk to the highway and wait for a bus, and I might be late." She added, as an afterthought, "Sunday morning is a busy time."

She watched the progress of the note from hand to hand, until at last it reached its goal. Dave read it quickly, then glanced her way, grinned, and made a circle of his thumb and forefinger, signaling his consent.

On Saturday night, instead of curling up in a corner of the living room to listen to the ski talk, Angela washed her hair and set it in loose pin curls before she went to bed. With her mother's tweezers she plucked a few straggling hairs from her eyebrows, and although she was so sleepy that she kept yawning and blinking over the task, she manicured her nails.

The next morning, however, she couldn't see that she looked so very different. Her hair was shining, it was true, and perhaps it framed her face more becomingly, but did it really matter, when a few hours from now it would be streaming in the wind?

There were twenty people for breakfast, some coming in from their rooms in neighboring farmhouses, because the fame of Mrs. Dodge's cooking had spread. They ate in two shifts, and Angela kept running back and forth from the kitchen with hot coffee while she kept an anxious eye on the kitchen clock.

The last straggler was out of the house before ten, but the stack of breakfast dishes still loomed large and an hour could pass like lightning, as Angela knew. "Next year," her mother said, "maybe we can afford an electric dishwasher." She was high-spirited this morning, because business was good.

Meanwhile, however, it was up to the two of them to get the dining-room floor vacuumed, the tables wiped and polished, the egg stains removed from the forks, and the dishes and glassware washed and dried and put away. Even working at top speed, this was a large order, and it wasn't surprising that Dave's jeep pulled up at the back steps while Angela was still up to her elbows in suds.

"You go on, dear. I'll finish," offered her mother generously. But Dave, poking his head in the door, said, "There's no rush. Give me a towel and I'll help."

He looked clumsy and out of place, standing beside the sink in his ski clothes, with a red knitted band covering his ears and a cowlick of hair standing straight up in the back. But he worked with surprising speed, and Angela was touched at his having offered. It put them on a different basis, somehow, and a new feeling of companionship warmed her as they jounced toward Bromley behind the drafty curtains of the jeep.

It was a perfect afternoon, cold but sunny, and although the slopes were crowded when they arrived, the week-end skiers began to depart about three and by sunset Angela and Dave had the place practically to themselves. The last run, as they came down the Twister toward the huddle of red buildings at the base of the mountain, was unforgettable.

Never had Angela felt such freedom, such confidence! Dave liked to ski fast, and she could follow him easily now, matching him turn for turn, flying in his wake like the tail of a comet.

"You're a natural!" he applauded. "You're good and you're going to be better." His earlier rancor disappeared in sheer admiration for her performance. "I bet you'll be racing before the season is finished. Another month and you'll have me completely outclassed."

"Oh, no," Angela murmured, but Dave's praise was as heady as wine. She drank in his words thirstily, for the first time discovering the pleasure to be derived from success. "Jacques says I've got to work and work and work," she told him. "I will, too! I think I want to ski well more than anything else in the world!"

I love it, I love it, I love it, her heart sang as they schussed the last stretch and skidded to a stop, side by side. Dave bent to loosen his bindings. "I'll buy you a hot chocolate," he said. "Boy, oh, boy, what an afternoon!"

Later, coming out into the early dusk, Angela glanced at her wrist watch and whistled boyishly. "It's a good thing this is Sunday and not Saturday," she told Dave. "Dinner is served at the Dodges' in exactly one hour."

"I'll get you home in fifteen minutes, maybe less."

"That's all right," Angela said. "Mother won't mind." She spoke, to her own wonder, with as much confidence as she skied. It was because she and her mother had reached a tacit understanding. Angela never let her mother down when she was really needed, and in return she was allowed special privileges whenever the work grew light.

Tonight there were only three guests left over from the week-end crush. Counting the Dodge family and Jacques, that made seven at the dinner table; but Angela noticed, the moment she entered the dining room, that it was set for eight.

"I thought Dave might like to stay," her mother suggested casually as she looked up from pouring milk into Chip's glass. She glanced toward the tall boy standing in the kitchen door. "How about it?"

Dave sniffed hungrily, recognizing a gingerbread odor coming from the oven of the wood stove. "I can't think of anything nicer. Could I call my folks?"

"Of course. The telephone is under the front stairs. But take your boots off in the kitchen. It's a rule of the house."

Bless Mother, Angela thought, for making it so easy. If she herself had ever considered inviting Dave Colby to dinner, she would have shied away from the thought as being overbold. Yet she was pleased that her mother had asked him on the spur of the moment. It was so obviously spontaneous, so unplanned between them, that the gesture seemed to be just right.

It was pleasant to be able to introduce Dave to Jacques and to the three guests, a family from Albany with a twelve-year-old son who was Chip's idol for the moment, because apparently he was more interested in setters than in skiing. She felt it gave her a certain prestige.

And Dave, for his part, acquitted himself well. He shook hands firmly, spoke to the adults politely, and listened to Jacques Brunner's comments on skiing with interest which gradually turned to trust.

Still red-cheeked and glowing from the cold wind, Angela felt completely at ease in the group around the dinner table. She smiled at everyone impartially and enjoyed the conversation which eddied around her, without feeling any compulsion to take part.

Then, as she slipped into her place once more after serving dessert, Jacques turned to her directly. "I saw you come down the Twister just before sunset. You were going very fast."

"Weren't we, though!" Dave broke in.

"He sets a mean pace," murmured Angela with a grin.

But Jacques frowned and shook his head. "For you I do not prescribe," he told Dave courteously, "but for Angie to ski very fast is not good right now." Once more he fixed her with his intent, serious eyes. "You must work to perfect your style," he said insistently. "Style! You understand? Let the speed come later."

CHAPTER *four*

"STYLE! You understand? Let the speed come later."

Because the words had taken the edge off her complete enjoyment of the day with Dave, Angela remembered them.

At first she felt a niggling resentment, because she liked to ski fast. She was good and she was going to be better! Hadn't Dave said she was a natural?

But out on the slopes, Jacques' appraising eye restrained her. His criticism could be sharp, his words cutting her down to size with the incisive quickness of a knife. From the Thanksgiving week end until the beginning of Christmas vacation, Angela schemed and fought for every possible hour of daylight she could spend at Bromley. She skied alone, mostly, but often at the bottom of a slope she would find Jacques standing and watching her. He seldom said anything complimentary any more. Instead, he rapped out instructions or censure like a drill-master, and finally Angela became indignant.

They were riding home from Bromley late one afternoon in the rattletrap car which Jacques had bought himself and which Angela now used as a means of transportation almost as much as he did. The highway was clear, but the back roads were icy and rutted and though he was driving very care-fully, still they skidded. There was no question of making faster time, so he had chosen this moment to give her a lecture on counterrotation.

"I'm not in training, you know," Angela snapped.

"Not in training? What do you mean?"

"I mean I'm not exactly going to try out for the Olympics!"

Jacques chuckled. "Not this year," he said. "But maybe some day . . ."

Angela glanced at his profile. "Don't be silly."

Jacques didn't take his eyes off the road, but he seemed to be speaking directly to the girl at his side, and Angela had the feeling that he was looking into her eyes, into her heart, perhaps into her soul.

"It is a possibility," he said softly. "A better-than-average skier at your age has every opportunity."

Angela felt a shiver trace its way up her spine. "Oh, now, Jacques!"

"It isn't a foolish thought," he said with sincerity.

"This year, next year, you work. Yes, you train!
You go into the local races. If you win, you go elsewhere. Onward. Then, who can tell?"

He seemed to be talking to himself, now, peering
into the night as though he could actually see ahead.
"When you drive a car and come to a corner, you
turn the wheel," he said, suiting action to words.
"It is as simple as that. The rest is judgment. You
judge how far and how fast to turn. Then you acquire experience. You learn what to expect of icy
roads, of gravel, of ruts, of hills.

"When you are an expert, skiing is very simple
too. The desire to turn registers as a motion of your
feet, fast or slow in this direction or that, depending
upon the slope. You turn the skis by rotating both
feet in the direction you want to go. The rotation is
made effective by keeping your weight even upon
both feet and making appropriate motions with the
upper body. The rest is judgment. When this be-
comes almost automatic, you can begin to practice
with the slalom poles. Then soon you can race!"

"Race?" Angela's heart pounded. "When will
that be?"

Braking as he came into the lane, Jacques smiled.
"I said soon, didn't I? Isn't that enough?"

Together they walked into the house, together
unlaced their boots and stored them in the alcove
behind the stove, where it was warm, but not warm
enough to dry out the leather. A pot of beef stew

smelled savory and inviting, the dining-room table
was set, but for once Mrs. Dodge was not in the
kitchen. She called a casual hello from the living
room, where she was reading a magazine in front
of the fire.

Chip was lying flat on his stomach, frowning over
some arithmetic problems, and Christie was curled
up beside him with his nose in the small of his
master's back. The scene was so domestic and
placid that it seemed very far from the world of
snow and speed and skill which Angela had just left.

She padded upstairs in her stockinged feet, with
Jacques just ahead of her. In the hall he stopped
and turned. "It is good to work hard for a goal,"
he said unexpectedly.

Angela didn't quite follow him. "A goal? What
goal?"

"We each have a different one, I think. You—to
race, to become an expert."

Because Jacques was already a pro, Angela looked
quizzical. "And you?"

"My goal is to bring Marie to this country," the
young Swiss said simply. "To be married and have
a place of our own." He gestured toward the grand-
father's clock on the landing and the old settle in
the upstairs hall. "Not grand like this, but three
rooms, perhaps." He grinned suddenly. "With
Marie that would be a fine home."

Angela shut the door to her bedroom softly, and

slowly changed from her ski pants to a skirt. "Grand," Jacques had said. He had called their farmhouse grand. It gave a whole new perspective to her life.

All that evening she looked with a sort of wonder at the beautiful old furniture she once had wanted to kick—even to sell! It was as though she were seeing it for the first time. Because their life in Vermont had been hard, it had never occurred to her to consider that for many people this would be a kind of luxury. It was her first introduction to the fact that everything was relative.

Later, when she was ready for bed, she put on a robe and went into her mother's room, needing to tell her how lucky she felt. Lucky to live in Vermont, lucky to have such a pleasant home, lucky above all to know that soon she would be good enough on skis to race!

"Race?" Janet asked. "Isn't it dangerous?"

Angela shrugged with complete fearlessness. "If you worry about it I suppose everything is dangerous—even crossing a street."

Her mother smiled. "You're a lot like your father," she murmured.

"Am I? How?"

"In personality. Charles loved to fly, I think, the way you love to ski. He said a flyer must have two prerequisites: skill—and courage. It takes courage to use skill, or to use it to the utmost. An error in judgment, a moment of uncontrolled fear—"

Angela hugged her knees, half listening, half dreaming of the future. "Jacques has made me practice and practice," she said. "Think of it! Without him it might have taken years to get to the place I'm in right now." Suddenly she leaned forward and threw her arms around her mother, anxious to express physically the exhilaration which buoyed her up. "It's such fun!" she cried. "Such wonderful fun!"

The fun showed in her face. Animation made her vivid, and it no longer mattered that she wasn't conventionally pretty, because the success she had found on the slopes at Bromley followed her to school. Dave asked her to stay for the dance after the next Friday-night basketball game, and Esther Byley gazed at her enviously from the side lines.

"You never told me," she complained, as they were doing dinner dishes together Saturday night. "You never even use lipstick, half the time. I didn't know you were interested in boys."

Angela laughed out loud. "I'm not, spelled with a capital *B*." She looked at her uninspiring companion slyly. "I'm interested in Dave, though. He taught me to ski."

Esther looked astonished. "He did? When?"

"Last year."

"So that's how you did it!"

"Did what?" asked Angela, puzzled.

"Got him to ask you for a date."

A date! She, Angela Dodge, had actually had a date. "A dance after a basketball game isn't exactly a date," she said, wanting to appear modest.

"Jean Parker thinks it is," Esther informed her, repeating gossip she had heard. "I understand she's furious."

"Oh, now!" said Angela. "There's nothing to it, really. Dave likes me, that's all. He used to wait for me to catch up on the ski slopes," she murmured reminiscently. "And now—"

And now, she thought with a sudden shock, *I wait for him!*

But Esther mimicked her. " 'He likes me, that's all.' " While Angela polished a dish absent-mindedly, Esther's expression turned sulky. "Not even any lipstick," she muttered. "It beats me."

It still "beat her" when Dave invited Angela to go to the Christmas dance. At first Angela hesitated. "I might as well be honest," she admitted. "I haven't got a dress."

Dave's reaction was heart-warming. "Phooey," he said. "What does a dress matter? Ask your mother. I'll bet she can dig something up."

Angela laughed at him in genuine amusement. "Digging something up won't exactly do, in this case. A dress may sound unimportant; but it never *is*, to a girl."

Still, she agreed to approach her mother, and Janet Dodge came through with a suggestion. "Would you trust me to make over that black-velvet dinner dress of mine? It has a lovely neckline, and if I took some extra darts at the waist I think it might be very becoming. At least you can try it on."

The dress was becoming—surprisingly so. Against the pastels worn by most of the other girls it looked almost daring, but its simplicity saved it, aided by the white gardenia which Dave brought in a florist's box on the fateful night.

"For me?" Angela did not try to conceal her surprise. She looked through the cellophane window at the flower on its bed of shredded wax paper, then took off the lid gently. "It's beautiful," she breathed.

Dave grinned and looked delighted when she lifted the creamy white blossom from its green nest and pinned it on. Her mother admired it too, and somehow it was just the proper send-off. Angela began there and then to have a wonderful evening, but she didn't guess that her thoroughly naïve pleasure in the corsage gave Dave the measure of self-confidence needed to spark the fun.

Not that she was a *femme fatale*, by any means. She was a merely average dancer, because she was unpracticed, but the co-ordination she used in skiing stood her in good stead and she was not heavy on her feet.

Occasionally she showed a tendency to lead, and about this Dave teased her. "Stop dancing alone," he commanded. "Follow me."

Angela flushed. "I'm sorry."

"Don't be," Dave said. "You're making out fine. You just need a firm hand."

"I'm so used to doing things by myself," she admitted.

"Too used."

"What do you mean by that?"

The sudden crispness in Angela's voice made Dave laugh. "You're independent as a hog on ice. You know that perfectly well," he said, and felt her back stiffen. "But," he admitted with frank admiration, "you're an angel on skis."

"An angel on skis." It was a light-hearted compliment, a silly remark to treasure, Angela told herself, yet she found that it made her work all the harder. She wanted Dave as well as Jacques to be proud of her. She wanted to live up to their expectations— and to her own.

Time, however, was at a decided premium. Because the snow was now six inches deep, skiers by the hundreds poured into the towns surrounding Bromley. From the morning after Christmas until New Year's Day the Dodge farmhouse was a bee-hive of activity. Every bed was taken, and two intrepid skiers even brought sleeping bags and commandeered the living-room floor.

"We never tripped over 'em before," Chip complained. "Christie can't even find enough room in this place to take a nap."

Angela worked beside her mother without complaining, but with secret fury, because the snow was so bright and so inviting, and because the two hours she took off every afternoon were so inadequate.

The lines at the lifts were long, the slopes were crowded, and instead of having fun she seemed to be struggling every inch of the way. More often than not she came back to the house exhausted, feeling that the time for which she had fought was wasted, and aware that the evening ahead would demand of her a quota of energy she did not have.

At this point Esther's chatter always seemed to be particularly insipid. Angela answered her in monosyllables, too fatigued to be more than civil.

"Don't you think Mr. Russell's sort of cute, for an older man, I mean?" Esther was referring to one of the guests.

"Mm-hm," Angela said.

"But his wife's too thin—*much* too thin—even if she does wear wonderful clothes."

"She was a model," Angela roused herself to mention.

"A model? Was she really? For fashion magazines, you mean?"

Angela shrugged. She didn't really know, nor did she care.

"I think being a model would be marvelous," Esther continued to burble as, with large red hands, she stacked the dishes Angela was carrying from the dining room. "But I don't know about ever being that skinny. Not the way I love to eat."

It was so patently ridiculous for Esther to put herself in Elaine Russell's place that Angela had to smile, but at the same time she was bored, insufferably bored. She wished she could work the magic in the old fairy tale, and say "Little goat bleat, little table away," to all the silver and glasses and dishes that would have to be washed and dried in the next hour.

"An artist's model wouldn't be so bad, maybe," Esther was continuing. She giggled self-consciously. "There was an artist lived over near Hapgood's Pond one summer. I heard him tell Mr. Peters, down at the post office, that he liked his models with a little flesh on their bones."

There was an endless spate of this sort of talk, until Angela felt ready to scream. She tried to divorce her mind from it, tried to answer without listening, but the words beat upon her with a steady, monotonous rhythm, and finally she could stand it no longer.

"Oh, for Pete's sake, Esther, stop talking!" she said.

The girl was reduced to sullen silence, but her bovine eyes looked so sorrowful that Angela felt contrite. "I'm tired," she confessed, "and I guess I'm getting edgy. I didn't mean to hurt your feelings. Forget it, please."

"The trouble with you is, all you want to do is be out skiing," Esther said awkwardly but with a certain amount of perception. "If you can't be skiing you're mad at everybody, including me."

Especially you! Angela wanted to shout, but she held her tongue, and later she even managed to say a pleasant good night. When she went upstairs she found Chip already asleep on a fold-away cot in her room, with Christie stretched out beside him, his red-brown head in the curve of his master's neck, and his legs stuck out stiffly, so that Angela brushed against them as she passed.

"You shouldn't be up there, boy," she whispered, but she didn't move him. Tonight it didn't matter enough. Within two minutes she had peeled off her clothes and tossed them on the nearest chair. For once there was something even more important than skiing—sleep.

CHAPTER *five*

ANGELA WAS PLAYING HOOKY. It was an unprec-
edented thing to be doing, especially with her
mother's permission; but here she was, looking down
from the top of the Shincracker, with Jacques Brunner beside her and the mountain so silent and
peaceful that they might have been alone in the
world.

It was Jacques who had cajoled Mrs. Dodge into
allowing Angie to skip school for the day. "Over
week ends I am always too busy to teach her. The
slopes are too crowded. What does one day matter?" he asked.

"My grades are all right, and we're only having
review anyway," Angie put in. It was just before
midyears.

"I want her to go into the Washington's Birthday
races," Jacques continued. "But she must have

more practice, especially for the slalom. It will be a problem for her, a test of skill."

"You think she is good enough?" Janet Dodge asked hesitantly.

"I know she is good enough," Jacques said.

So here they were, standing on the very top of the mountain, on a Tuesday morning when not another soul had yet come up the lift. Accustomed to seeing the trail beribboned with ski tracks, Angela gazed down at the new powder with a rising sense of anticipation. Frost had turned its surface into crystals which glittered in the sun like diamonds, and she knew exactly the light swishing sound her skis would make as they lifted the snow in a scintillating cloud.

"Ready?" Jacques asked, pushing off with his ski poles.

"Ready!" Angela called, but waited a few seconds to give the instructor a head start.

Then, with the rush and sparkle of a Vermont freshet, she swooped down the mountainside behind him, mimicking every turn, every downhill run, keeping to the path Jacques carved.

She could see, even as she sped downward, how expert Jacques was in choosing the exact and fastest line. Ahead of her, he cut corners with the utmost precision, and the snow flew up behind him in feathery wings. He never skidded, never sideslipped; he looked self-confident and relaxed. And as Angela followed him, trying to match his speed, she realized what a beautiful performance she was watching, and how much she wanted to be a pupil of whom he could be proud.

At the bottom of the slope Jacques waited for her. "Fun, wasn't it?" was all he said.

"Marvelous fun!" Angela agreed. "It's the first time we've ever had the mountain to ourselves. It's like owning the whole outdoors!"

After two more trial runs Jacques let her go ahead. "Imprint on your mind each curve, each bump, each obstacle," he told her. "This is the course. Learn it. Ski it that way. And climb the run at least once before any race. There is no better way to survey the terrain and select the shortest and best line."

Once more they met at the bottom of the slope, and this time Jacques sent Angela up on the lift alone. With one of his ski poles he signaled her to start, and at the command Angela pushed off powerfully, taking a few skating steps to increase her getaway speed. This, she knew, was the real test, because at the bottom of the course Jacques was timing her. Faster, she drove herself, faster! Watching the trail which was now broad and clear, she skied nonstop to the imaginary finish line.

"Good!" Jacques called, and figured the time. "Let's rest, now, and have lunch. This afternoon I will set up some slalom gates."

Angela agreed reluctantly. She didn't feel at all tired. But as they ate the sandwiches Mrs. Dodge had packed and drank the cocoa Jacques bought, she realized that she had been keyed up to a fever pitch, and that her legs really needed a rest.

For half an hour after eating they sat side by side on a bench on the south side of the shelter and loafed. Jacques talked in his precise, rather pedantic English, as usual about skiing. "It is the fearless racer who wins the downhill," he explained, "but it is the technician, the prudent runner who never loses control of his skis, who triumphs in the slalom."

"I'm not afraid," said Angela, pondering the difference.

"No, you're not," Jacques agreed. "Often you ski with the verve and courage of a man."

Angela glanced up at him, not sure that this was a compliment. "Is that bad?"

"It is good," Jacques said. "But you must remember that a watch-tick moment of bad judgment, a split second out of control can send you off the course at a fatal sixty-mile-an-hour clip!"

"I can't ski sixty."

"You will," said Jacques.

It was a promise. More than a promise, it was a vote of confidence. Angela knew that he liked to teach her, that the snow bunnies and intermediate skiers with whom he spent most of his working time were far from a challenge to his capacities. He gave her free of charge his very utmost; he held forth to her like a gift his every skill.

She liked Jacques, even felt a sort of hero worship for him, because he represented near perfection on skis. He talked to her on many different levels: like a pupil, like a member of his adopted family, like a friend, and sometimes like a woman and a confidante.

She knew, by now, all about Marie, whose name sounded so delightfully French, because he accented the first syllable. She knew how much money Jacques had saved, how firm were his intentions, how high his hopes. "She will like Vermont," he said. "She will miss the Alps, the really high mountains and the wide-open slopes. She will miss the background music of the cowbells and the almost breath-taking beauty of our country, but she will understand the people here. They have dignity, like the Swiss."

"Are the Swiss so very dignified?" Angela teased.

"I think so," Jacques replied seriously. "It has been said that men grow to match their mountains." Bending, he started to tighten his bootlaces. "Enough philosophizing. We must get to work!"

He set up five series of flags along an empty slope, and explained to Angela—as though she didn't know!—that the gates set vertically on the hill were called blind or closed, while those set horizontally were known as open gates. "A series of three or more blind gates is called a flush," he added, "but this you will not attempt today!

"Don't race against time," he cautioned her. "It is much more important to establish rhythm, to practice technique and precision. When these become second nature to you—and only then—you are ready to be clocked."

Angela was an indefatigable pupil. She would have worked until sundown, but at four o'clock Jacques stopped her. "When you are tired," he cautioned, "you become tense, and it is then that the accidents occur." He took her home in his shabby little car, which coughed and sputtered angrily because it was cold. "Take a hot bath and a nap," he advised her. "You have come a long way today."

Though there was no more time off from school, Angela managed to manipulate her schedule so that on two afternoons a week she could break away early and catch the mail bus which passed Bromley. Here she got off and hurried to Jacques' car, where her boots and skis were stashed. Since she was already wearing her ski pants, it was a matter of minutes to change in one of the shelters, and then she had time for two hours of practice before darkness fell.

Whenever possible Jacques joined her. By late afternoon the novices had left the slopes and none but the most ardent skiers remained. These were few and far between on weekdays, so Angela's opportunity to practice was unimpeded. Sometimes a few grosbeaks sitting on the branches of the pine trees were her only audience.

Jacques, drumming away at basic rules, found his *protégée* quick and responsive. He taught her the fine points of control, illustrating the sideslipping caused when a racer over-edges his skis, and emphasized again and again the importance of getting the weight forward.

Angela could feel the amount and force of her body rotation change continually as she skied the slalom courses Jacques mapped out. Each was more difficult, more intricate than the last, but she welcomed the challenge. It was like a wonderful game to prove her skill, and she loved the knowledge that she was developing individual style. Often she was laughing in sheer delight as she skied up to Jacques at the finish.

In order to get experience in actual competition, she entered the weekly standard races and placed well. Of course she was far from expert. She skidded and fell again and again, especially when a sharp turn was necessary. But she always picked herself up and was off again like a flash, undismayed. She knew the placement of the flags wasn't responsible for these occasional mishaps. It was she herself who was not yet equal to the task of weaving in and out at such headlong speed.

"But I will be!" she told Jacques, and she could see that he believed her. "I love it so!" she cried, exhilarated. "Nothing else in the whole world is so much fun."

Fun. Sheer, unadulterated fun. It was the word she always used in her mind when she thought about skiing. It was the way she felt these days, and it showed in the readiness of her smile, in the unaffected sparkle of her dark-brown eyes.

Mrs. Dodge, recognizing the lift which accomplishment was giving her daughter, made no mention of the times when she was overworked because Angela shirked her home duties. And Angela, in her turn, felt the strength of her mother's interest and support, although she was living too completely in a world of her own to be aware that she was frequently neglectful.

Chip, a year older now, a year wiser, operated on the fringe of both his mother's and his sister's worlds. Christie was a dog, no longer a puppy, a companion rather than a baby animal to be cuddled and loved. His coat was burnished copper with the sheen of silk velvet, and his muscles moved under the skin in a way which even Angela, self-absorbed as she was, found beautiful.

Once in a while Chip approached his sister with

a question. "Did Daddy ever have any guns?" he asked one day.

"I don't think so. Why?"

"I'd like to learn to shoot," he said. "After all, Christie's a gun dog."

Angela was waxing her skis. She looked up and sat back on her heels. "What would you shoot—birds?"

Chip looked a trifle disturbed. "Not pheasants," he assured her. "I couldn't kill a pheasant, I don't think."

"What could you kill? Quail? Grouse? Woodcock?"

"I don't know." He glanced at Christie dubiously. "Do you think setters have to hunt to be happy?" he asked.

Angela wasn't sure, but she was beginning to understand Chip's dilemma. He didn't want to hurt anything, but at the same time he wanted to do right by his dog. "Christie looks happy enough," she told him.

Smiling, Chip said, "Maybe I'll just shoot clay pigeons then."

Another time he came to her with the suggestion that perhaps she could teach him to ski, but the problem of acquiring equipment was too much to cope with. Angela could see that his heart wasn't set on the idea. He dropped the subject quickly

and went out to throw a stick for Christie to re-
trieve.

There was a thaw and then a quick freeze during
the first week in February, and the slopes at Bromley became icy and hazardous. Angela skied with
proper caution, but even so she had trouble edging
properly, and on her turns she kept sideslipping, in
spite of anything she could do.

"Your skis," Jacques said in some concern, "just
aren't good enough."

"They're all I have."

"I know. I know. Stand next to me," he said, and
measured their shoulders. "How tall are you,
Angie?"

"Five-six, I think."

Jacques shook his head. "You're more than that."

It turned out she stood five feet six and a half
against the instructor's five-nine. Because she was
so slender she looked taller, but it was impossible
for them to exchange skis. "Mine aren't right for
racing anyway," Jacques admitted. "I told you
that. When the time comes I'll try to get you a
better pair from the rental shop. Don't worry. Keep
practicing on those."

On the Saturday before Washington's Birthday
Angela managed to get away from the house especially early. Her mother, going marketing in
Manchester, gave her a ride to Bromley, and Angela
arrived in time to avoid any wait at all for the lift.

The day was cloudy, with the top of the mountain lost for ten minutes at a time in mist, and the runs were peopled almost entirely by skiers who would be contesting against one another in the holiday races. To Angela, observing them critically, they looked far more expert than herself.

This was partly because of their equipment. She noticed the famous names on the skis, the razor-sharp offset edges which she knew by now were essential for the slalom. She was aware of the hand-made boots from Austria or Switzerland, boots which fitted their owners like fine gloves, allowing no ankle wobble such as she had to contend with constantly.

She felt like a sparrow among a flock of peacocks, but her eyes were level as she sized up her competition. She would do her best; to do more was impossible, so why worry? Slipping off the lift at the top of the slope, she skated over to the down-hill course.

There were a few figures dotted on the snow field below her, experienced skiers, taking it easy, getting the lay of the land. Angela adjusted the straps of her ski poles, pushed off, and went flying down-ward, schussing for a few seconds in the sheer joy of speed, then practicing her turns by cutting in and out among the pine trees on a track she knew by heart.

"Look out!"

The warning, so unexpected, so loud and close, threw her out of control for an instant as she went into a swivel-hip turn. She glanced sideways at a young man who stood in the shelter of a tree. Off balance, her skis twisted, and she suddenly found herself lying in the snow at his feet.

"Sorry. I thought you didn't see me."

"I didn't," admitted Angela, unhurt. "Your parka blends right in with the trees in this mist."

He stretched forth a pole to help her up, but she scorned it and was on her feet in a twinkling, brushing herself off.

"Not much of a day," the boy said conversationally. He was tall, Angela noticed, six feet or more, and he had the most engaging gray eyes she had ever seen, beneath heavy dark eyebrows with a rakish, almost Mephistophelian tilt.

Angela squinted at the clouds. "Nope."

The lad laughed. "Spoken like a true Vermonter."

"I'm not a native, though."

"Oh? Up here visiting?"

"No. We've moved here from Philadelphia." How did I get into this, Angela wondered as she stood talking. But she made no move to push off. There was something compelling about this strapping fellow, an easy-going masculinity that combined brawn with charm.

"I watched you come down from the top," he said. "You're good."

Angela, swiping a mitten across the back of her pants, looked rueful. "You mean I make good sitzmarks."

The boy laughed again, and she looked up at him, trying to estimate his age. Eighteen, possibly nineteen, she suspected. She wondered where he went to school.

"Racing on Tuesday?" he asked unexpectedly.

For some reason Angela didn't want to commit herself. "Maybe," she said.

"You must be a Vermonter!" he insisted. "At least you have all the earmarks. I'll bet you're racing, and since we'll probably meet later anyway, I might as well introduce myself. My name's Gregg Harrison."

"Hello, Gregg," Angela said with a smile.

"Aren't we going to play tit for tat?"

"I'm Angela Dodge. I live up the road, near Peru."

"Magnificent. Two whole sentences! We're making progress. Now if we could ski down the rest of the way together, we might become fast friends."

His nonsense made Angela laugh. She liked him. Who could help but like him? But some perverse impulse made her push off.

"Wait for me!" she heard him call.

Wait for him? In a few seconds he was past her, skiing with a hell-for-leather dash which swept him down the dizzying descent in spirals as graceful as a dancer's. Crouching, straightening, getting every possible bit of speed out of the snow, he made Angela actually feel his power, his certainty.

At the bottom of the hill when she pulled up beside him, breathless with admiration, she said something so utterly artless that it was a supreme compliment. "I think you're wonderful!"

CHAPTER **six**

GREGG LAUGHED. "I was just showing off, actually.
I'm no better skier than you."

"Oh, yes, you are!" Angela's tone of voice per-
mitted no contradiction, because she knew he was
just being polite. With unusual boldness she asked,
"Where do you go to school?"

"Dartmouth. I'm in my first year."

"I might have known," Angela murmured, impressed. "I think if I were a boy that's where I'd
want to go."

Gregg looked at her inquiringly. "For the skiing,
you mean?"

Angela nodded.

"You've got it bad, huh?"

"I guess you'd say so."

"We're two of a kind," Gregg said. "How old
are you?"

"Almost sixteen," Angela fibbed, wanting him to think of her as more grown-up than she really was.

"You'll be great, some day," Gregg told her. "Anybody with the start you've got—"

"How about yourself?"

The boy shrugged. "We'd better move over to the lift, hadn't we, and get in line."

They skied together all morning, without any prearrangement, but just because it seemed the most natural thing in the world to do. Angela felt for this stranger an affinity which transcended anything she had ever felt for Jacques or for Dave. They seemed to suit each other's mood, to have an almost psychic understanding of one another's ambition. And beyond this was something new and strange and stimulating. Whenever she stood close to Gregg or looked directly into his eyes, she could feel her blood race; she could feel a disquieting thrill.

This disturbed but excited Angela. She was certain that Gregg looked on her merely as a chance companion, friend for a morning. After all, he was a college man, and she was just a kid.

But he doesn't know I won't be sixteen until next fall, she told herself. He won't have to know. She was sure she looked older—could act older, if necessary—and she began to wish with sudden passion that she had paid more attention to her appearance; that she had remembered to put on lipstick after breakfast, that she had made a serious study of the techniques by which to attract a boy. It mattered —it mattered terribly!—what Gregg thought of her. She wanted him to like her, not as a skiing companion but as a girl.

In a lesser way she had felt this once about Dave, but his mere physical presence had never made her tremble. He fed her ego when he asked her to the Christmas dance, but he didn't arouse in her any violent emotion. Next to Gregg, Dave might have been made of papier-mâché, he seemed so unsubstantial. Gregg was solid. Gregg was real.

With the fiery vehemence of youth Angela tried to deny what was happening to her. There was no such thing as love at first sight. She'd read about it in books and pooh-poohed it as novelists' nonsense. Anyway, she was too young.

But what is too young, she wondered. And why should I think this devastating emotion—not entirely pleasant—has anything to do with love? She knew only that she felt overeager and uncertain, transported and at the same time let down.

Would she, Angela wondered with a feeling of panic, ever see Gregg Harrison after the races were over? How could she make him *want* to see her? How did girls arrange such things?

Noon came, the hour at which her mother was to pick her up. The sun burned through the haze and the snow glistened, but Angela was scarcely aware that the weather had changed. On her last run down the mountain she skied with abandon, neither knowing nor caring whether she kept on course. Jacques greeted her at the shelter with a frown on his face. "What's the matter with you?" he asked. "You're all over the place today."

Angela made an inconsequential reply. She was looking around for Gregg, who appeared at her elbow without warning. "Hi there. I lost you," he said.

Angela introduced him to Jacques. "I have to go. My mother's waiting for me," she said unhappily.

" 'By then. See you tomorrow?"

"I expect so." She tried to keep the remark casual to hide the excitement which had turned her hands to ice.

In the parking area Mrs. Dodge was fretting. "You're late," she said a trifle sharply. "Ten minutes, one way or the other, are important on Saturdays."

"I'm sorry," Angela murmured, but there was no conviction in her voice. She sat slumped in her seat until they reached the house, replying to any comment requiring an answer in the most perfunctory manner, and neither knowing nor caring how many guests were expected to arrive by sundown.

Gregg. Gregg Harrison. A strong, spirited name!

Gregg continued to haunt her every thought as the day wore on. She counted the hours until morn-

ing, when she might see him again. She catalogued
his features, his straight nose, his wide-set eyes, the
tilt at the corners of his generous mouth. She tried
to imagine what his life was like at Dartmouth, and
because of him, the college acquired for her a
romantic aura.

"Angie, the napkins."

"Yes, Mother?"

"You've set the table without any napkins."

"Oh, all right."

A few minutes later, sent down cellar to fetch
something from the freezer, Angela stood before
the open box for three full minutes, unable to
remember what the something was.

Finally she called upstairs. "What did you want
me to get?"

"Three cartons of frozen string beans."

"Oh, yes." She spoke vaguely, and almost forgot
a second time.

Instead of moving quickly and with decision, she
wandered in and out of the kitchen like a somnam-
bulist, completely lost in a daydream. "What on
earth are you mooning about?" Chip was sagacious
enough to ask, but Angela didn't even hear him.
She was wondering whether Gregg had a girl.

He must have a girl, she thought. A boy as attractive as he is! Jealousy stabbed her. What was
she like? Blonde? Petite? Pretty? She imagined

her to be soft and kittenish, even cloying. Everything which she herself was not.

"I bet she can't ski worth two cents," she muttered to herself.

"What are you grouching about, Angie?" It was Chip again.

"Nothing." Indeed nothing! A mythical creature, a figment of her own fancy—yet possible, even probable—a girl of whom she must beware.

"Angela. Please. Wake up!"

"Sorry, Mother. What did you want?"

"The water. I asked you to fill the water pitcher."

"I will."

But she continued to move through the routine tasks as through a fog. Indulging in fantasy wasn't at all her nature, and her mother looked puzzled and rather provoked; but Angela didn't notice. Gregg, she kept repeating to herself. Gregg Harrison. Such an exciting name!

Whenever Angela wanted to look her best she always washed her hair. Therefore she washed it again tonight, although it was only three days since her last shampoo. Setting it under the rather dim light in her own small bedroom, she examined her face in the mirror and wished desperately that she were prettier and that she had more of that illusory thing which girls called sex appeal. She went to bed but not to sleep. Wide-eyed, she lay thinking.

How can I attract him? How can I make sure that he'll want to see me again?

They were questions which Angela was incapable of answering, and she knew it even as she pondered them. What did she know about boys, really? Nothing. What did she know about Gregg Harrison? Very little. That he went to Dartmouth and that he could ski. Skiing was their only bond.

Very well. She'd start from there. If she could ski so well on Washington's Birthday that she earned his admiration and respect, wouldn't that be something? Not enough, perhaps, but something. It was her only hope.

In the morning she was heavy-eyed but determined. If she had worked hard before, at Jacques' behest, she would work doubly hard to prove herself to Gregg.

Only one thing deterred her—Gregg himself. He appeared around the corner of the shelter while she was clamping down her ski bindings and said, as though they had never parted, "Hurry up. The snow's perfect at the top right now."

"I've got to practice," said Angela without much conviction.

"Practice along with me."

But it wasn't practice when she was with Gregg, and Angela knew it. She let herself go, and skied without worrying about speed or thinking too much about the course. Another morning went by with a jet plane's whoosh, and the only personal remark Gregg made was, "What have you done with your hair?"

"Just washed it."

"It's different. You curled it."

Angela nodded.

"I liked it better the other way," Gregg said.

How can you please a man, Angela wondered. How can you possibly know what to do?

In different circumstances, and at another time, she would have asked her mother, but over this week end Mrs. Dodge was too busy to be bothered with a teen-age romance. Angela sensed this, and also realized that actually she didn't want to talk to anybody about Gregg. Her feeling for him was too urgent and too private. This was something she'd have to work out alone.

Yet a sense of inadequacy nagged her. She had none of the tricks of a girl like Jean Parker. She knew none of the wiles. And even her skiing seemed to get out of control as the day wore on.

Jacques shook his head when he saw her and came over to give her some advice. "Better knock off for the day, Angie. You were skiing like a bird this morning, but now you're trying too hard."

She nodded, knowing that he was right. But how could she quell the tenseness which was building up inside her? How could she explain to Jacques that she had to impress Gregg in the Tuesday races, that unless she outdid herself and came in a winner she felt sure she would never see him again?

That night she brooded. Going through her accustomed chores automatically, without any real interest in serving the guests or joining in the conversation, she was scarcely aware of Esther Byley's monologue, which was interrupted every time Angela left the kitchen, then continued again on her return.

"You're a queer one," Esther commented from the sink, where she was up to her elbows in soapsuds. "Don't you care?"

Angela didn't answer, because she didn't know what the girl had been talking about.

"I said, 'Don't you care?'"

"I'm sorry," said Angela without any conviction. "I wasn't listening."

Esther sighed. "I was just telling you that Dave Colby has started to date Jean again."

"That's his affair, isn't it?"

"Well, I just thought you'd be interested, since he took you to the Christmas dance."

Angela frowned. If she had failed with Dave how could she hope to succeed with Gregg? To her mother's helper she said, peevishly, "Oh, Esther, dry up! Can't you ever think about anything but boys?" Then she felt like a hypocrite, because what had she been thinking about all evening herself?

The next day she counted it fortunate that Gregg

did not show up at the slopes until afternoon. All morning she worked with furious concentration, determined to be in top form for competition on the following day. She knew Gregg would be in the college races, while she herself would be in a quite different class, but nevertheless she wanted her record to be one on which he could congratulate her. Hadn't he said, on first meeting her, that she was a good skier—that some day she might be great? This she would have to prove tomorrow, for herself and for him!

Jacques, cutting his lunch hour short, timed her on the downhill. "What are you mad about?" he asked when she swung to a halt in a swirl of snow.

"I'm not mad," she told him.

"You look it. You ski as though you were furious."

Were determination and fury then such similar emotions? Angela shrugged nervously. "How many seconds?" she asked.

"Don't fret about the time. Relax, Angie. I told you yesterday, you're trying too hard."

Angela didn't believe him. She couldn't try too hard, for Gregg. When he appeared an hour later, she felt her knees turn to jelly, and she begged off skiing with him on the grounds that she had been practicing all morning. "I've had it," she said, "for today."

"Come on then. I'll buy you a hot chocolate before you go home." Leading her into the Wild

Boar, he found an empty table. "I had to drive my uncle in to Bennington," he explained. "What a wasted morning!"

"Are you staying with your uncle?"

Gregg nodded. "Mother and Dad are away, so I came here for a long week end. Anyway, I thought the races might be fun."

Over their steaming cups of chocolate Angela learned a little more about him. He came from Boston and had gone to preparatory school at Vermont Academy, where he had been on the ski team. Now he was jumping for the freshman team at Dartmouth. "That's my real interest," he admitted. "Though I like slalom racing too."

"What about the downhill?"

"That I could live without. Mere speed doesn't fascinate me. I like tests of skill."

Angela nodded understandingly. She felt the same way. "I'll look forward to seeing you tomorrow," she said.

"And I you."

It was the knowledge that Gregg was watching the next day that made Angela so nervous that she trembled visibly as she waited to start her slalom run.

"Ten seconds!" called the starter.

Angela took a deep breath and tried to steady herself. Butterflies in her stomach flapped wings that seemed uncomfortably real. Did all racers feel like this?

"Five . . . four . . . three . . . two . . . one . . . go!"

Driving hard, she swung out of the slot against her outthrust poles. Below her the gates looked like a maze, and the snow was crisscrossed with the runners who had gone before her.

Where should she check? Which was the best line from one gate to the next? Slashing through the first open gate, she tried to judge the lay of the land, using the knowledge of slopes and fall lines which Jacques had so painstakingly taught her.

A third of the way down the course she shaved a flag and arced right in too fast a turn. Down, she cautioned herself. Down! A slight check, a left swing, a right, another left. She was in the corridor before she knew it, going with such speed that, out of control, she overshot the next gate and went into a cartwheel which landed her on her stomach.

I'm through! I'm finished!

She couldn't blame it on the rented skis. They were good—sharp-edged and far better than the ones on which she had practiced. Up on her feet in a second, she finished the course, but she had wasted precious seconds and she knew she was out. Her time would be hopeless.

Jacques broke free from a group of instructors watching their pupils perform and said, mildly reproving, "Tough luck, Angie."

"This is an off day," she admitted.

Jacques nodded. "Steady down."

But she couldn't steady down, not now. She came in eleventh on the downhill, when she knew Jacques expected her to place third or fourth. Her lungs ached and tears stung her eyelids, but she winked them back. She felt thoroughly frustrated, because she knew that on any of a dozen practice runs she could have beaten her own time.

"Forget it," Jacques urged, as she handed over her racing bib. "Go watch the college crowd. You'll see some good skiers." But he looked after her with a concerned expression as she poled off to join the spectators gathered at another slope.

CHAPTER $\wr$ *seven*

IT TOOK EVERY BIT of courage Angela possessed not to cut and run.

She wanted to get home, to hide herself away with her disgrace. When she had tried so hard, when she had wanted a thing so much, it was shattering to realize defeat. Gregg, if he had seen her race, would be completely disillusioned. A fine skier indeed!

Great was the word he had used. "Some day you'll be great." What an utterly ridiculous remark.

She chided herself remorselessly, beating herself with scorn as a whip. She examined the dream which had sustained her for the past year and told herself that it was made of something so unsubstantial that, like a snowflake held in the palm of her hand, it melted under scrutiny.

No matter how good her time was when Jacques

held the stop watch for a practice run, or when she skied against local talent Friday afternoons, if she couldn't stand up in open competition it didn't count. Where was her control, where was her speed, where was the pure joy of skiing which had been hers when she met Gregg last week?

Biting her lip, she bent down and unfastened her bindings, then slung the skis up over her shoulder and joined the crowd watching the college racers tick off the seconds in the downhill.

These were the experts, the lads who might even be Olympic material. From Middlebury and Norwich, the University of Vermont and Dartmouth they had come, and Gregg was among them, somewhere up there on the mountain, waiting his turn to slide forward into the slot.

She saw them start, one after another, as their time was called, but she couldn't pick out Gregg at this distance. She didn't recognize him until he was past the upper S turn and breaking into the straightaway, riding close to the woods on a high line, snow swirling in his wake.

Then it was by his style that she knew him. He was running well, low-crouched to avoid wind resistance, and he met the bumps and twists of the course with poise and undiminished speed. There was a breath-taking schuss at one point, and she could almost hear his skis singing. He did a mambo step to avoid a rock, and she gasped in admiration.

"Go, go, go! But watch those ice patches!" she wanted to shout.

Now he was on the flat, bearing down on the final schuss full tilt. He shot through the finish line and swung to a halt, grinning. He knew—and she knew—that he had made every second count.

Yet there were others even better. When the times were all in he placed fifth, with a time of one minute, ten and two tenths seconds. What a shame, Angela thought, after such a beautiful run! But Gregg didn't seem to be disturbed in the least. She could see him in a group of racers, all wearing numbers, and he looked just as relaxed and genial as ever when the announcement came over the loudspeaker.

Didn't he care?

If she had been able to speak to Gregg she would have asked him this question, but already he was moving over to the lift, and the slalom was being announced as the next event. She had to find her own answer, and it didn't take long. Hadn't he admitted that downhill was not his dish, that he was a slalom man and a jumper? Then he was even more expert than she had suspected! A hot flush crept to her cheeks when she thought of all the times he had waited for her, pretending that he was no better than she was.

Angela found a vantage place on the hillside from which to watch Gregg make his first slalom run.

He came over the knoll at wide-open speed, took a four-gate flush with swivel-hipped ease, and swept on down the dizzying descent with great style, checking at the last possible moment, squeezing the gates one by one, and coming straight in over the finish line as though he'd enjoyed every second.

Ah-h, thought Angela, with a true athlete's admiration. Smooth, very smooth. Then envy pricked her. If only she—!

She didn't wait to see him make his second run. She couldn't, because time was running out and she had promised to get the rented skis back to the shop. Returning them, she felt as though she were handing back a ticket to paradise—a paradise which she would never know.

It hadn't occurred to her that she wouldn't see Gregg to say good-by. But now it didn't matter, really. He'd be on his way back to Hanover tonight, the youngster he had picked up at Bromley forgotten. Or if he remembered her at all, he'd decide that you couldn't spot a comer by seeing a person ski for fun. It was competition that counted, competition in which judgment and speed and skill combined to prove a skier's worth.

That night, for the first time since the week following her father's death, Angela cried herself to sleep. She wept for the chance she had missed, for the dream which was ended, and somehow it all became entangled with the fact that she had never seen Gregg to say good-by.

And now I won't ever see him again! Or if I do it will be when he's skiing and I'm standing on the side lines, the way I was this afternoon, and he won't even know I'm there. But if I could have won that race he would have remembered me. He would have looked me up, or called me, or *something*. She was sure of that.

Sobbing, she let herself go in a paroxysm of self-pity. Nothing ever came out right, nothing! It didn't matter that this was her first important experience in racing, that the next time she might do better. The thing was, that here and now she wasn't quite good enough.

Turning her sodden pillow, Angela punched it angrily. She was so heartbroken and confused that she couldn't decide which was more important, skiing or Gregg, because they had become inseparable in her mind.

For the rest of the week she lived within a veil of misery which neither her mother nor Jacques could penetrate. The temperature rose and a false spring sunshine melted the snow on the mountains, leaving patches as bare and brown as Angela's mood. She felt so choked up and wretched that she could scarcely swallow, and her appetite became so poor that her mother fretted.

"Maybe you need a tonic, or some vitamin pills."

But it wasn't a tonic Angela needed. She knew that. In spite of herself, Gregg filled her thoughts and she kept looking anxiously for a letter which she knew wouldn't come. "I'm all right," she kept insisting. "Don't worry about me." But the gloom which enveloped her was so contagious that it affected the entire household; even Christie regarded her with mournful eyes.

Over the following week end it rained, churning the back roads into rivers of mud. Angela brooded in her room, pretending to study, but actually staring out at the dripping trees in discouragement. Loving action as she did, the dead stop to which her life had come was more than she could face.

I'll write to him myself, she decided, and went down to the desk for some note paper. "Mr. Gregg Harrison, Dartmouth College, Hanover, N. H.," she wrote on the envelope. Would that be enough of an address to reach him? She'd have to take the chance.

Then she stared at the blank paper for a long time, pondering what she could possibly say that would be light and casual, that wouldn't give her true feelings away.

"Congratulations on a wonderful performance," she wrote finally. "I'm sorry I couldn't stay around to say good-by."

It sounded a trifle stilted, but she couldn't do any better. She sealed the letter and walked with it

through the rain to the R.D. box before she could
change her mind. It's not such a terrible thing to
do, she thought. It doesn't require an answer. But
she could always hope.

Hope raised her spirits a trifle, and a change in
the weather brought four inches of new snow.
Jacques invited her to meet him at Bromley after
school on Thursday afternoon. "Before the week-
end rush," he said, and added, "they're going to
roll the slopes today." He always chuckled when he
made an announcement like this, because in Switzerland, where he had lived, such a process would be
unthinkable. To go over the Alps with a power-
driven roller would seem as absurd as manicuring
a cow.

"I'm not sure I can," said Angela, without meeting
his eyes.

In contrast to her usual enthusiastic reception of
such an opportunity, this was so negative that
Jacques turned and asked, "Why?"

"Well . . ." she fumbled, searching for a logical
excuse.

Jacques' eyes became keen. His jaw line firmed.
"There's one thing I never thought I'd have to call
you, Angie," he said coldly. "A poor sport."

She glanced up at him, stricken, but he gave her
no quarter.

"I'll meet you at three-fifteen at the usual place."

She stood completely still, unable to answer.

"You'll be there?"

"Yes." The monosyllable was almost a whisper. Angela felt as though he had struck her. She almost wished he had. At school she crept through the corridors, avoiding any of the casual contacts she had come to enjoy, and her classmates looked at her strangely. What was wrong with Angela Dodge?

"A poor sport." The phrase ticked over and over in her mind like a metronome. Poor-sport, poor-sport, poor-sport. It was a stigma she couldn't live with. By noon she knew that she would have to go out and do her best to disprove it. She would have to give this task her utmost. She would have to fight!

Jacques was waiting for her, his expression more kindly. "You know the expression, 'One swallow doesn't make a summer.' Well, one race doesn't make a skier. The Franconia races are coming up a week from Saturday and I want you in them. Remember that." He patted his pupil on the shoulder. "Now go on up there and show me what you can do."

Angela gritted her teeth. "Don't think I won't try!" she muttered, and hurried over to catch the lift.

Pushing off on her downhill run, her face was grim. This was no longer a game; this was a job— something she had to lick. She skied furiously, with intense concentration, going to the top again and again while Jacques held the stop watch, but somehow she never seemed to better her Washington's Birthday speed.

"O.K.," he said finally. "That's enough." Driving home together, they didn't talk much. Angela was bone-tired, but still tense with effort, and Jacques didn't seem to have anything in particular to say. But when they pulled in to the turn-around, he cut off the ignition and twisted sideways in his seat.

"Let's forget what I said about the Franconia races," he suggested. "As a matter of fact I think you'd better quit racing for the rest of the year, Angie. You're trying too hard. You've lost the fun of skiing, somehow or other. And you're the sort of person who can't ski really well unless you're having fun."

It was true. She knew it was true, but it still made her sick at heart. Tramping into the house in her heavy boots, she felt as though she were a hundred years old. All sense of expectation was gone.

Then her mother picked up two letters from the clutter of envelopes on the kitchen table. "One for you, Angie, and one for Jacques. Everybody's lucky today!"

Lucky, Angela thought, is scarcely the word. But at that moment her eye was caught by the postmark. Hanover!

She took the letter upstairs to read it, clumping through the house in her boots in spite of her mother's protest. "This once it doesn't matter," was all she said.

Sitting on the edge of her bed, still in her outdoor clothes, she took off her mittens and ran a finger under the flap very slowly. She was almost afraid to discover the contents. "Please God," she prayed silently, "let it be all right." She couldn't stand another disappointment today.

"Dear Angie," Gregg had written, "It's been a while since I got your nice note, but I've been trying to jack up my grades so they won't chuck me off the freshman ski team.

"I looked for you after the Bromley races, but you had disappeared. Saw you in the slalom. You showed a lot of style until you got going too fast. Take it easy, girl! Skiing is a sport, not a business. Have fun until I see you again. Best, Gregg."

Until I see you again. Angela's heart leapt. What did he mean by that?

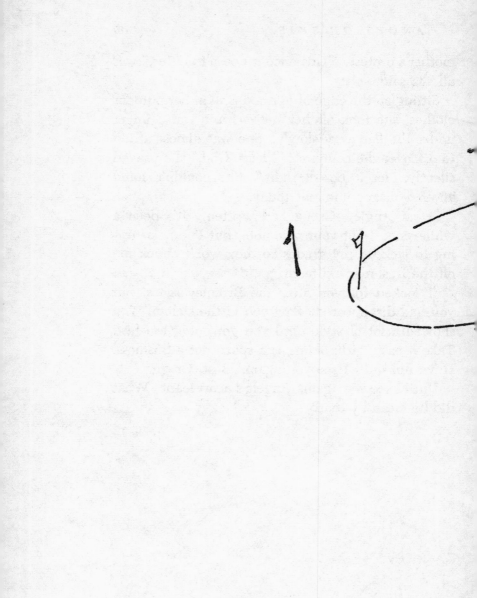

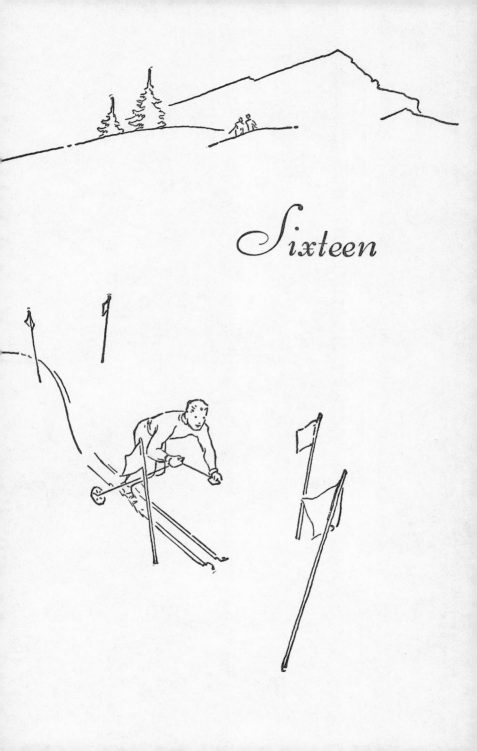

Sixteen

CHAPTER   *one*

"UNTIL I SEE YOU AGAIN."

These were the words Angela remembered. This was the phrase she repeated in her heart. She couldn't know that it had been written lightly. She treasured it, hugged it to her, and as a result Gregg's warning to take it easy passed almost unnoticed. Only vaguely was she aware that he was saying, in different words, what Jacques had told her in much stronger terms.

Skiing, as a matter of fact, no longer dominated Angela's waking thoughts. She put it from her, turned her face the other way when the school bus passed Bromley, and told herself that she was finished, that she had failed.

Without recognizing that she was doing so, she replaced her dream of skiing with a dream of Gregg. Although she would have denied vigorously that she

191

was in love ("But I scarcely know him!" she would
have said), Angela once more began to wander
through the school corridors in a fog.

Spring came to Vermont almost imperceptibly
that year, or perhaps Angela didn't notice, in her
trance, that the vaselike elms and massive maples
were greening, and the birches were topped with
feathery pastel leaves. She wrote Gregg several
brief notes and received replies that were quick,
inconsequential scrawls, for which she sometimes
had to wait for weeks, but they heartened her.
"Until I see you again," he had said!

"Again" was long in coming. The Hendersons
returned to their remodeled house, bag and bag-
gage, the children plump and rambunctious, eager
to see Angie, eager to go swimming, although the
water was still icy cold. "Are you still willing to
baby-sit?" Mrs. Henderson asked, and Angela
smiled and said, "Of course."

It seemed as though she moved through a familiar pattern, but that she herself was a shadow and
did not belong to it. She walked the sun-dappled
roads with feet that scarcely touched the ground
and she felt depressed and elated by turns.

In June, right after school closed, Mrs. Dodge
began the construction of a new bunkhouse for
skiers. It was an adjunct of the barn, really—an
extension building typical of Vermont architecture,

and both Dave and Ted Jameson were hired to help the carpenter.

They arrived with lunch pails in the morning, just before eight o'clock, looking scrubbed and healthy and remarkably grown-up to Angela, who usually was clearing away the breakfast dishes while her mother was out discussing plans with Mr. Makin, a whiskery old gentleman in coveralls who had a reluctant admiration for the shrewdness of Janet Dodge.

It was Mr. Makin who had remodeled the house some years before; it was he who fixed the tractor when anything went wrong; and it was he, along with Mrs. Dodge, who had drawn up the plans for this new addition to the place. "Don't need an architect with a woman like your mother," he had informed Angela. "Horse sense, that's what she's got. Mighty rare, these days."

It was a long speech and a great compliment, coming from a native, and Angela remembered it as she saw the building grow. The boys were good workers and seemed to enjoy the job, hoisting and sawing and hammering with good-natured attention to Mr. Makin's instructions, while Mrs. Dodge, assisted by Jacques, who was earning his board by helping about the place, worked tirelessly in the truck patch nearby.

Angela, by nine o'clock, was off to the Hendersons and her "fearsome foursome," as she called the

children. She found time to chat with the boys only
in the early morning and late afternoon, when they
met on terms of casual friendliness. The Christmas
dance was the last date for which Dave had ever
asked her. After that his attentions had returned to
Jean Parker. Apparently skiing, Angela concluded,
was their only real bond.

Once in a while they arranged a picnic supper,
with Barbara Benton and Jean and Ellen Whipple
and some of the others in the school crowd. They
usually went to Hapgood's Pond, because it was
handy, and because the water lent a certain en-
chantment to the setting sun.

It was at one of these suppers, quite unexpectedly, that Angela again met Gregg.

She hadn't heard a word from him since the end
of school, but he still occupied her thoughts; and
when he cantered up beside Barbara on a chestnut
mare, Angela shook her head in spontaneous dis-
belief.

She was sitting on the grass beside a picnic
hamper, sorting paper plates and napkins, and he
didn't see her at first. Barbara swung down from
her saddle and introduced him to Dave, who was
coming across the road from the jeep with a couple
of cartons of soft drinks in his hands, and then to
Ellen and Ted.

"I've brought along an extra guest. Hope there's
enough to eat."

Ellen looked up at the newcomer and batted her eyelashes becomingly. "Do you like fried chicken?"

"Do I!" Gregg grinned engagingly.

A stab of jealousy made Angela flinch, and half a dozen questions crowded one another. When had he come? How did he know Barbara Benton? Why hadn't he written her? Not that he had any obligation, actually . . .

Sitting cross-legged on the grass down near the pond, she realized that he hadn't noticed her yet, but when he did his head lifted in surprise. "Angie!"

She looked up. "Hi, Gregg." Her voice sounded small.

Tying his mare to a sapling with a quick half hitch, he hurried toward her. "Hi! It's good to see you. How've you been?"

Not quite meeting his eyes, Angela said, "Fine."

Gregg squatted on the ground beside her. "You look fine," he said, and she was unreasonably glad that she had worn her yellow Bermuda shorts and a clean striped shirt which matched them.

"Are you visiting your uncle again?"

The boy nodded. "Just drove down this afternoon."

"I didn't know you knew Barbara Benton."

Barbara came up behind them. "I didn't know Gregg knew you."

Gregg stood up and put an arm across Barbara's

shoulders. "We played in sand piles together, girl. My uncle's place is right next to hers."

"Oh." Angela felt slightly mollified by the explanation, but the gesture made a tight knot develop in her chest.

"Come on, people!" called Dave from a distance. "If we don't swim now, we'll have to get out our ice picks." There was a splash, then a yelp, and a thrashing of long arms and legs.

The rest of the crowd changed into swimming suits and joined him for a dip, then came out shivering and toweled themselves dry, refreshed and hungry. Angela almost avoided Gregg, because she wasn't quite sure of her status, but he brought his plate and sat down beside her on a car robe.

"How was the spring skiing at Bromley? Good?"

"Fair," Angela replied noncommittally. "How about Hanover?"

"Wonderful! We were lucky this year."

Dave, who was sitting across from them, stopped munching a chicken leg, and asked, "You ski?"

"A little."

"He skis," said Angela flatly. "He's good."

"Look," broke in Barbara Benton. "It's summer now. Remember?" She glanced toward the half moon appearing in the sky on the opposite side of the pond. "Couldn't we get a little more seasonable?"

Everybody laughed, but Gregg looked at Angela.

"In Chile," he remarked, "there's skiing right now. Wouldn't you like to be there? I would!"

Angela looked at her plate and shrugged slightly. "I didn't do much skiing after that week end with you," she confessed, under cover of the others' conversation.

"Well, why not?"

"I don't know."

"Lose your nerve?" Gregg pressed.

"Not exactly."

"What, then?"

"I don't know. I can't explain it," she said, frowning.

"Look at me."

Angela glanced up, her eyes troubled but honest.

"I believe you," Gregg said. "We'll discuss it some time."

Dave was looking at the pair of them curiously, as though he wanted to get into the conversation but didn't quite know how. For the rest of the evening he watched Angela covertly, and the next morning he asked her quite openly, "Who is this guy Barbara had along last night?"

"This guy Barbara had along." Jealousy stabbed afresh, but Angela managed to keep her expression calm. "You heard his name—Gregg Harrison. I met him at Bromley last winter. He'll be a sophomore at Dartmouth and he's a darned good skier. Made the freshman team."

Dave whistled softly. "He must be good!" Then
he added, "You seemed to know him pretty well."

"Not really. We skied together a couple of days.
That's all."

"What about Barbara?"

"What *about* Barbara?" Angie repeated.

"Is he going around with her?"

"I don't know." She hoped she didn't sound as
miserable as she felt.

The conversation was interrupted by a shout
from Mr. Makin—"Get a move on, lad!"—but Angela
pondered the question as she started down the road
to the Hendersons'. Although Barbara and she were
friends, she felt grudging and suspicious; and her
temper was not improved as the pair trotted by on
horseback in midafternoon, when she had taken her
charges on a hike up Styles Mountain and was cutting back to the Hendersons' by way of a bridle
path.

Recognizing her, they pulled their horses in and
stopped to chat. "I didn't know you ran a kindergarten," teased Gregg from his saddle.

"I didn't know you rode horseback," Angela
retorted, "until last night."

The boy grinned down at her. "I'm a learner,"
he said. "Barbara's the expert."

"Every man to his own sport," Angela murmured
with a shrug.

"What's the matter, Angie? You sound . . . upset," said Barbara, as though she were vaguely concerned.

"Oh, really?" Angela forced a smile. "Sorry. I didn't mean to. Maybe"—she glanced down the path at her four charges—"it's kindergarten fever." But she knew in her heart that this had nothing to do with the case.

Gregg dropped by late the same afternoon. He and Chip were sitting on the top step of the back porch examining a shotgun when Angela arrived home from the Hendersons'. Dave and Ted had already left and Mr. Makin was just backing his truck out of the parking area, so there was no background noise of hammering and sawing to disturb the country peace.

Walking with deliberate slowness, although her heart leaped at the sight of him, Angela approached. The two were in deep conversation, Gregg's eye sighting through the barrel, Chip gazing at him in rapt admiration, unconscious that his sister was anywhere around.

Suddenly Gregg lowered the gun. "Hello there!" he called. "I thought for a minute you were a new kind of bird."

Angela grinned. Such nonsense was always infectious when it came from Gregg. There was something about the rakish tilt of his eyebrows above those remarkable eyes which captivated her. "I feel like a crow, hoarse from cawing," she said, and dropped down on a lower step. "Why the gun?"

"It was Dad's," Chip explained, as though she hadn't known that it had been around the house for years. "Gregg was just looking at it, to see whether it was O.K. for me to handle."

"You?" Implicit in the syllable was the fact that Angela considered him a baby, far from old enough for such talk. Chip stiffened aggressively. "Maybe," he told her, with a level glance and outthrust chin, "he'll teach me to shoot."

"How old are you, Chip?" asked Gregg, intervening.

"Eleven," said the boy proudly, without mentioning that his birthday was only a few days past.

Gregg nodded thoughtfully, weighing the gun in his hand as he did so. "This seems a bit on the heavy side, but Uncle Henry has a Fox Sterlingworth .410 over at the house that we could borrow."

Chip's eyes shone, but he asked, a bit apprehensively, "What would we shoot?"

"Tin cans, at first, until you learn to hit a moving target. Then clay pigeons, if I can scare up a hand trap."

"Mr. Nickerson might loan us his," suggested Chip.

Angela was feeling completely left out. "You'd better ask Mother's permission first," she warned.

"I will, right now!" Chip agreed, jumping to his

feet. He vaulted off the steps and raced around to the other side of the house.

"Good boy, your brother," commented Gregg, when he had disappeared.

"He's got a dog complex," said Angie.

"I know. We've talked about it. If I owned Christie I'd be pretty proud of him myself." He leaned forward and said dreamily, "I've always wanted to have a good gun dog."

Angela turned on the step and clasped her knees. "You certainly are a person of varied interests!"

Gregg smiled. "Did you think skiing was my only love?"

Angela looked startled. "I guess maybe I did."

"Because it's yours?"

She was silent for a moment. Then she rested her chin on her knees and answered without looking at the boy on the step above her. "But it isn't," she said. "As a matter of fact, I think I've given it up."

"Angie!" Gregg sounded completely astonished. "You're kidding!"

"No, I'm not kidding," said Angela slowly, but she felt suddenly cold and wretched, although the day was warm.

CHAPTER *two*

GREGG STAYED at his uncle's farm for ten days, and
during that time Angela and Barbara shared his
attentions, but skiing was not mentioned again until
the very last evening.

He took Barbara to the movies, then Angela to a
barn dance, and along with the school crowd all
three went on a hay ride. In between times he was
just "around."

Chip found in Gregg a new hero. He hung on his
every word, followed his instructions carefully, and
was delighted when Gregg complimented him on
his quickness in learning to handle a gun. Angela
watched her young brother pick up several Harrison mannerisms, heard him discuss blue rocks with
a man-to-man air, and noticed that he was holding
himself with Gregg's erectness, shoulders well back,
stomach tucked in.

Meanwhile, as she learned to live with the jealousy she could not overcome, Angie hung on Gregg's words with a devotion almost equal to Chip's. When she was with him she felt completed and at ease; she forgot Barbara. When she was away from him she counted the hours until she might see him again.

During that period, although she was quite unaware of it, Angela blossomed. Her skin took on a new glow, her eyes became brighter, her hair more glossy. Even her mother commented on it. "You know, my pet," she said one morning at breakfast, "you're getting positively pretty."

Angela flushed. "Me? I'm too tall and gawky."

"You were gawky last year. Now you're willowy. There's a difference."

It was a new and fresh kind of beauty that Angela was acquiring. She had the slender figure of a nymph, and she walked with an easy grace. Her face revealed its good bone structure, strong but feminine; and when she forgot to use lipstick it didn't really matter, because she had enough natural color of her own.

On the last night of his visit Chip—not Angela—invited Gregg to dinner, and they all cooked steaks on the outdoor grill. Jacques and Gregg discussed skiing with great animation, to Chip's secret disgust, and Gregg said, "You should see the Dartmouth Carnival. That's the thing!"

"I'd like to, but I am saving money to be married, and it is expensive to take a trip."

"When are you going to be married, Jacques? You've been talking about it for a year and a half now." Chip spoke with boyish forthrightness.

"Soon, I hope. I have almost enough. Next month I shall write Marie, and perhaps she will come by Thanksgiving." Jacques' face became animated at the very thought.

"Where will you live?"

"I'm not sure yet. In the village, probably. Then she may find work at one of the inns."

"You mean she'll work?" Chip sounded so shocked that Angela was embarrassed, but her mother burst out laughing.

"What do you think the rest of us do?" she asked.

"Gregg doesn't work," Chip announced proudly. "He goes to Dartmouth."

"Hey there!" Gregg objected. "I wait on tables for my board, boy! Just because I go to college doesn't mean I'm rich."

"You mean I might go to college some day? Me —or Angie?"

"Why not?"

Why not indeed, thought Angela, as she sat and listened to the conversation which eddied around her. There were scholarships, student loans, jobs to be had. A person who really wanted something could usually get it. She'd like to go to Middlebury, where there would be skiing—

Skiing! She stopped, astonished at the turn of her own thoughts. Hadn't she told Gregg she'd practically given it up?

But she hadn't told Jacques, and she didn't. Time enough in the fall, or in the early winter, when the leaves had fallen and winter's soft, blanketing whiteness was again on the mountains. Time enough, when Gregg was back at school and this feeling of excitement had died within her, when she was again herself.

That night, after Chip went to bed, she and Gregg walked up the road to the beaver dam and found the little builders working in the moonlight. They didn't talk, for fear of disturbing them, but stood in the shadow of a clump of pines and watched them. And again, as on that first day when they had skied together, Angela felt for Gregg a sort of rapport, a like-mindedness that was very special and peaceful.

On the way home he kissed her good night.

It wasn't an urgent caress, not even a very romantic one. He simply stopped by the fence and turned her toward him, holding her shoulders. "You're a nice girl, Angie," he said. "I like you." Then, quite as though it was the most natural thing in the world to do, he bent and gently kissed her lips.

For the next three days she walked on air, buoyant with the memory, Barbara's rivalry forgotten. Then she settled down and lived through the rest of the summer, waiting for a letter or a telephone call, though neither came.

"Have you heard from Gregg?" Barbara asked her bluntly on the first day of school.

"No," said Angela. "Have you?"

Barbara shook her head, and they both laughed thinly, then went about the business of signing up for sports and filling out schedules. Burr and Burton, no matter if the sky fell, would apparently go on.

And in a way, in spite of the nagging wish that some word would come from Dartmouth, Angela found it pleasant to be a junior. Upper classmen had a certain prestige. Moreover, she now felt quite secure in her group of friends.

Dave, who had been graduated last June, was still working as an apprentice carpenter with Mr. Makin and waiting for the draft board to call him. He fell into the habit of dropping in at the Dodges' over week ends. The bunkhouse was finished, with a carved Swiss balcony designed by Jacques, but there were towel racks to be put up and storm windows to be fitted and all sorts of odd jobs to do, and he used these as his excuse.

But actually, as Angela gradually became aware, she herself was the inducement. Ever since Gregg appeared on the scene, Dave had looked at her with new eyes, as though she were a specimen plant, hidden in a wealth of greenery, which somehow he had overlooked.

He asked her for dates—definite dates planned a week in advance, not just casual invitations to the movies. Sometimes she accepted; sometimes she didn't. Now that it didn't matter, it seemed a very easy matter to attract Dave.

On her sixteenth birthday he brought her a box of candy, and she was sincerely touched. "How very nice of you to remember!" she said.

"Why wouldn't I?" he asked, shuffling his feet a little, like a country boy.

"I don't know. You never did before."

"You were never sixteen before."

Sixteen! It had a singing sound. It seemed a lovely age to be. Angela smiled and thanked him very warmly, but she knew that a card from Gregg would have meant more than ten boxes of candy from Dave.

Yet in spite of this persistent silence it was a pleasant autumn. The harvest was plentiful, the freezer full, the house in shipshape order for the first of their winter guests; and Janet Dodge, though lean and tough as a day laborer, no longer looked worried about keeping the wolf from the door.

The first snow came early in November, a real blizzard which lasted for two days. Instantly the

phone started ringing. "Long-distance, Mother!"
Chip called again and again as reservations poured
in from Albany, from Boston, from New York.

Jacques waxed his skis and rattled down the road
toward Bromley, where the lifts were already running, and Angela and her mother made up a dozen
beds. "Isn't it wonderful!" exclaimed Mrs. Dodge
happily. "At last we're really rolling. I must call
Esther Byley and see if she can come back."

Esther could come. "I'd be glad to," she said,
and sounded as though she meant it. When she
arrived late Saturday afternoon she was positively
beaming. "I've missed all the excitement around
here," she said.

"Excitement?" Angela didn't quite understand.

"The comings and goings and. . . . Well, it's
different," she finished lamely. She went to hang
up her coat and scarf, then asked when she came
back into the kitchen, "Is Mr. Jack still here?"

"Jack? Oh—Jacques!" Angela repeated, automatically correcting the pronunciation. "Yes, indeed." She showed her the chalet-type bunkhouse
with its picture-postcard balcony, and Esther exclaimed in admiration.

"My!" she kept repeating. "My!"

Mrs. Dodge, who had been rolling out dough for
raised rolls, told some stories about its construction,
and Esther began, in her slow-moving way, to clear
up in her wake.

"I do believe you're getting thinner," Mrs. Dodge observed after a few minutes, and Esther replied proudly, "I am. I've lost eight pounds."

Her skin was improving too, Angela noticed, although she didn't mention it. The adolescent acne was disappearing, and although Esther would never be handsome she was no longer repulsive. She looked ample and comfortable and pleasant—country qualities which Angela was learning to appreciate.

The skiers stamped in, cold and wind-burned and hungry, the hearty, happy people who were a breed to be found from Stowe to Sun Valley, wherever there was snow. Angela's heart instinctively warmed to them, and she served them cheerfully, once more filling her ears with talk of "moguls" (as they termed the bumps), of techniques, and of the merits of various trails.

"I'll drive you down to Bromley if you like, Angie," Mrs. Dodge offered as they put away the last of the breakfast dishes. "I suppose you're positively bursting to get out!"

Angela shook her head. "I don't think I'll go skiing today," she said without emphasis.

Janet Dodge's head snapped around and she looked at her daughter in amazement. "What's the matter? Don't you feel well?"

"I feel all right," Angela said, and sought for an excuse. "I have a lot of homework, that's all."

But her mother knew as well as she did that this wasn't an honest answer. She felt a reluctance she couldn't explain, almost a fear. Instead of the heady enthusiasm which she had known so well there was an emptiness inside of her, a concern that she might not show up well, that Jacques—that Gregg!—would be ashamed of her.

She got out her books and was turning the pages of her history notes when the telephone rang. "Will you answer it, Angie?" her mother called.

"Hello," she said.

"Hi. Angie? This is Dave. Get into your boots. I'll pick you up in fifteen minutes. The snow is wonderful!"

A thrill leapt, unbidden, within her; but she quenched it. "I'm afraid I can't. I've got stacks and stacks of homework," she said.

"Nonsense. You're on the honor roll for the first marking period. You told me so yourself. Be ready, because I'm coming right over!"

"Dave!"

But the receiver clicked and the line was dead.

Angela turned away from the instrument slowly, and a dozen remarks began to haunt her. "A poor sport," Jacques had called her. "You've lost the fun of skiing." And Gregg had written, "Take it easy, girl. Skiing is a sport, not a business." Her hands felt cold and clammy, her throat tight. She walked into the dining room, where her mother was sorting silver, and said, "Dave's coming over. He expects me to go skiing and I don't want to. What can I do?"

"*Why* don't you want to go?" Mrs. Dodge asked. She put the last of the knives and forks in their compartments and met her daughter's eyes with a level, questioning glance.

For the first time Angela answered truthfully. "I'm scared," she said.

"Scared of what?"

"I don't quite know." Angela frowned.

"Are you sure you don't know?" Janet's eyes were both tender and sympathetic, but they were also direct.

We are two women, faced with a problem, trying to find an answer, her expression said.

And meeting her mother this way, on equal terms, Angela could search her own heart without embarrassment. "I think," she said slowly, "I'm scared of being not quite good enough."

Suddenly, gushing from an unsuspected source, the words were spilling over. "Jacques expected so much of me. He thought I'd make a *great* skier. He said so. And I've let him down."

"Because you didn't win the first race you ever ran, Angie? You haven't let him down, dear—yet."

"But I don't want to be seventh-best!" Angela wailed. "Or second-best, if it comes to that."

Janet Dodge smiled very gently, and slowly

shook her head. "Sometimes," she said, "the second-besters make the nicest people—not because they have won, but because they have learned how to lose."

Angela dropped her eyes and looked at her clenched hands, without being aware of her own tension. "You think I ought to go, then?"

"I *know* you ought to go."

Yet neither of them moved.

"There was something else Jacques said," Angela told her mother, and tried to recall his exact words. "He said I was the sort of person who can't ski really well unless I'm having fun. Do you believe that?"

"Do you?" Mrs. Dodge asked.

"I guess maybe."

"You used to have fun, didn't you?"

"Oh, yes!" Angela's head came up, and her eyes were alight.

"But you don't . . . any more."

"Not the same way. It happened right after I met Gregg. I guess Jacques was right. I began to try too hard."

"Why? To impress him?"

Angela's eyes grew dark and troubled. "I never thought of it that way, but he's so terribly good. Oh, Mother, you should see him! He skis like—like a bird!"

Mrs. Dodge smiled again. "The whole trouble

with you, darling," she suggested lightly, yet confidentially, "is that you might be just a little bit in love." Then, with one of her typically quick gestures, she came over and hugged Angela to her. "Hurry!" she commanded. "Get into your ski things. I'll tell Dave you'll be right down."

CHAPTER ╳ *three*

MONDAY, this early in the season, always seemed very quiet, with the slopes at Bromley almost bare, the week-end crowds departed. Angela looked out from the school bus at the bright red buildings and the flying flags of the skiing nations and said to herself, "Well, I did it. I got out there. But I certainly wasn't much good."

She had skied with unusual caution yesterday, letting Dave take the lead, following in his wake—the tail to his comet as he swooped down the trails. And he had seemed to enjoy himself hugely, glad to be in the ascendancy once more, making much of his prowess and teasing her for being "chicken" on the moguls.

"You ski your way. I'll ski mine," Angela told him tartly. "I don't want to break my neck the first time out."

214

She was stiff this afternoon, which wasn't surprising. Even soaking in a hot bath last night hadn't helped much. Remembering her rigorous training of two seasons ago, she dog-trotted along the road toward the farm, breathing as Jacques had taught her. Up one gradual rise, down another. Panting, she slowed to a walk and shifted her books. It would take a while to get in shape.

The trunks of the trees were very black against the snow, and the evergreens supported white pillows along their branches. There was a wind which now and then rubbed saplings in the woods together, making a sound like the twang of an off-key violin, and every once in a while a snow pillow fell with a soft plop.

How very familiar it all was, Angela thought. How familiar, and how dear. Philadelphia seemed very distant, and far from distinct in her memory. Yet this would be only her third winter in Vermont.

A bridge crossed the road, and a brook where she and Chip had fished for trout last summer snaked its way darkly between alabaster banks. The birches rose like silver pencils and the farmhouse, with Jacques' jalopy parked in the drive, looked snug and homey in the distance. Unconsciously, Angela began to hum.

She was still humming when she went into the house. On the kitchen table was a hasty note from her mother. "Chip and I have gone to Manchester

for new shoes. Guess whose? Back on the late side.
P.S. Please set table and stir stew."

Hanging her coat in the hall closet, Angela went
upstairs to change her shoes. As she unearthed the
pair she wanted from the muddle on her closet floor
she paused, listening. From the adjoining room,
which was Jacques', came a strange, muffled sound.

Someone—not a child but an adult!—was sobbing,
with a racking, desperate attempt to keep from being heard. Angela stood completely still, shoes in
hand, shocked to the very core. Was it—? Could
it be—?

Acting without any thought of propriety, completely on impulse, she tiptoed back to the hall in
her stockinged feet, went to Jacques' closed door,
and opened it gently, turning the knob without
making a sound. The young man lying face down
on the bed didn't hear her. His head was cradled
in his arms and his shoulders were heaving in a
losing fight for self-control.

It was the first time in her life that Angela had
ever seen a man cry, and her stomach knotted in
compassion. Quickly and silently she crossed the
room and sat down on the bed, leaning forward to
put her arms around his shoulders, her cheek against
the back of his head.

"Jacques—Jacques," she whispered, suffering for
him. "What's the matter? What is wrong?"

There was no answer. Jacques shook his head

silently, and as though Angela's discovery of his weakness came as the final blow, he became shattered by sobs.

"Jacques, Jacques dear," Angela kept murmuring, and stroked the back of his neck with her fingers, as she would have tried to comfort a child. Wildly she thought, I'm not old enough! If only Mother were here.

But there is a time in every girl's life when she must behave like a woman, and this was it for Angela. There was nobody to call upon in the empty house, and she was faced with a disaster as to which she could only guess.

"Is it . . . Marie?" she asked gently.

Still unable to speak, Jacques nodded violently.

"Is she"—taking a deep breath she forced herself to speak the word—"dead?"

In answer the young man held out a letter crumpled in his right hand. Angela took it and smoothed it out and walked with it to the window.

"But I can't read it! It's written in French."

Still, with her schoolbook knowledge of the language, a few words and phrases were familiar. ". . . *se marier . . . mon époux . . . avec regret . . .*"

The meaning hit Angela like a blow between the eyes. "She—she has married someone else!" she said, horrified. There was no denial. This, of course, was it.

In one instantaneous moment, a fraction of a

second out of time, Angela tried to relate this crush-
ing blow to her own life, to identify herself with
Jacques. What if she heard that Gregg was engaged
to be married? What if she knew that she would
never see him again?

And yet, by comparison, this was a minor tragedy
she was imagining. Angela knew, in the most
minute detail, the fervor with which Jacques had
worked and saved, the good nature with which he
had attacked any odd job which would bring in
extra money, the great joy with which he had looked
forward to the day when he could board the bus
for New York City and meet Marie at the dock. If
I had her here, she thought, I'd throttle her! How
could a woman be so perfidious, so ignoble, so base?

Suddenly her voice cracked like a rifle in the
supercharged atmosphere. "Jacques!"

The unexpected sharpness of tone made the
young man's sobs shudder to a halt; his head was
still buried in his hands.

"Jacques, you've got to believe this. Now listen!
You're lucky. You don't know it yet, but you're
lucky!"

This startled him into a response. "Lucky? Ha!"

Angela came over to the bed and forced him
to sit up and face her. Could she find the words to
make him see the truth? "If she could do this to
you she isn't the girl you thought she was. Don't

you see? In a woman without loyalty, what do you have? What kind of marriage would it be?"

"I—I love her," Jacques muttered.

"You love the girl you thought she was," Angela insisted, her eyes burning. "You don't love the girl who couldn't wait, who didn't care enough to bide her time."

Jacques shook his head, denying her statements, but he listened.

"I know," said Angela firmly, "that if you'll just pull yourself together and *think*, you'll agree with me."

She belabored him with this argument. She prodded and pommeled and pushed relentlessly, asking him what sort of wife a girl like that would make, asking him whether a person who couldn't be loyal for two years could remain faithful for a lifetime, asking him to examine himself, to discover whether he was brokenhearted over a girl or a dream?

She found words she had never used before, dredged up from her subconscious for this particular emergency. For half an hour she talked and questioned and made Jacques answer, and when she left him she knew that the worst was over, that somehow she had given him the insight and the courage to face facts.

Then, having met disaster head on, having weathered the storm, Angela's knees turned to water, and she grabbed the rail to keep from falling as she went downstairs.

The back door slammed just as she reached the dining room, and her mother burst in along with Chip and Christie, all three normal and noisy and full of high spirits.

"Did you stir the stew, Angie?"

"I will."

Stir the stew. Set the table. Such trivial things they seemed, after the emotional tempest through which Angela had just been dragged; but she did them, and they calmed her.

When she and her mother were alone in the kitchen she whispered the bad news. "Mother, Jacques has just had a terrible shock. Marie has jilted him and married another man."

"Oh, no!"

Angela nodded, and felt herself begin to tremble. "He's—he's been crying, Mother. I've tried to do what I could. But is there any way we can keep Chip quiet without telling him? You know how transparent he always is."

"I'll see what I can do," said Janet. She looked stricken. "The poor boy," she murmured to herself.

"Maybe he'd rather have supper upstairs to-night," suggested Angela after a few minutes.

"We'll see."

But before they could suggest it, they heard

Jacques come down and go out the front door, wearing his ski things. He started up the lumbering road, trudging along slowly, and both Angela and her mother watched him from the window.

"Don't worry," her mother said. "He's just going for a walk."

He came back late for dinner and ate in the kitchen, helping himself from the stew kettle. Tactfully, Mrs. Dodge arranged to get Chip to bed early, and Angela, exhausted with strain, took her books and went upstairs at the same time. But later, awakening from a restless sleep, she could hear the murmur of voices from the living room, a man's deep baritone intermingled with a woman's softer tone.

Bless Mother, she thought. If anybody can help him, she's the one. It didn't occur to her that the most essential medicine for Jacques' malady had already been given, that through her own doctoring the cure had begun.

It seemed to Angela that the rest of the week passed with leaden slowness. Jacques was silent and preoccupied, Chip was engrossed in a book of dog stories one of the skiers had brought him, and her mother was going about her affairs with a determined effort to be cheerful and keep the household on an even keel. By Friday morning Angela was ready to welcome the usual week-end bustle, because at least it would offer a leavening touch, a change of pace.

But the temperature had risen, and the rain which had pelted on the farmhouse roof Thursday night covered the mountains with frozen fog. Every hill was topped by pale ghostlike armies of trees, and the slopes at Bromley looked slippery and uninviting as the school bus skidded past them.

In the first-floor corridor at Burr and Burton Angela passed Barbara Benton on her way to history class and stopped to borrow a book which she had forgotten and left at home.

"By the way," Barbara said lightly, "I had a letter from Gregg, at long last. He's skiing madly and thinks he'll get a chance at some competition jumping in the college meets."

"Really? How marvelous!" Angela replied, trying to sound bright and pleased, and doing her best to keep her face inexpressive. Why had Gregg written to Barbara and not to her? Did that mean . . .?

"He's on some committee or other for the Dartmouth Winter Carnival. I can't remember exactly what," Barbara went on.

She can't even remember. I'd remember! Angela thought. The mere mention of the carnival made her heart drop with a sick thud. Had he written to invite Barbara, then? It was awfully early, but she knew that the boys lined up their dates for the big week end months and months ahead.

"When is the carnival?" Angela asked in order to say something—anything.

"Sometime after Christmas. I'm not sure of the exact date."

The flare of jealousy burned a bit less brightly. If Barbara couldn't remember the date, then surely . . .

"You'll return that book after study period, won't you?" Barbara was asking.

"Of course. I'll bring it to you in math class." About to turn away, Angela suddenly noticed a pin fastened to Barbara's sweater and leaned forward to examine it.

Barbara giggled. "I was wondering if you were blind, Angie."

"I just saw it." But she still couldn't make out the name of the school.

"It's Ted's, of course. Didn't you know we were going steady?"

Angela grinned, relief surging through every vein. "I am blind, I guess. Since when?"

"Since September."

The second bell rang, making them scamper in opposite directions, but Angela called over her shoulder, "See you later, Barb!" with a lilt in her voice.

Ted Jameson. Imagine!

But of course the confession was still no proof

that Gregg Harrison hadn't written to Barbara, quite unknowing. . . .

Outside the temperature began to drop again, and by midafternoon there was an inch and a half of fresh snow.

CHAPTER *four*

"WHAT'S THE MATTER with Jacques? He seems awfully glum," said Esther, with more astuteness than Angela would have suspected she possessed.

They were alone in the kitchen, finishing the Saturday-night dishes, and from behind the closed door could be heard laughter and conversation from the living room, but the creaking of floor boards above their heads told them both that Jacques had already left the group.

"I guess now's as good a time as any to tell you," said Angela, lowering her voice. "Marie, the girl he was engaged to back in Switzerland, has married another man."

Esther's pink hands, polishing a glass, stopped moving, and her limpid brown eyes acquired a sympathy which was also expressed in her voice as she said, "Oh, you don't mean it, Angie!"

"I wish I didn't."

"Why, the poor fellow. He's too nice, much too nice. . . ."

She paused, and Angela said, "That's the way we all feel."

"I wonder if he'll stay—or go back?"

"Go back to Switzerland? I doubt it. He likes the United States."

Esther sighed, and put down the glass she was drying. "I don't see how a girl could do such a thing," she said. "Especially not to Jacques Brunner. Why, just to look at him you'd know they don't come any better. Is he taking it hard?"

Angela nodded. "I guess you'd say so. I wish he'd find somebody—anybody—to go out with. Even to the movies in Manchester. He just sits up in his room and broods."

She carried a stack of breakfast plates over to the warming oven and slid them in, then turned back to Esther, who was again standing motionless, her face flushed with perturbation. "Do you think," she asked after a long moment, "if I had Mom invite him to Sunday-night supper at our house, he'd be willing to come?"

Angela almost burst out laughing, the suggestion struck her as so unlikely. Yet she controlled herself. Esther was utterly serious, and she was only trying to do something nice, something to help.

"I don't know, but I guess it wouldn't hurt to ask."

"It might make him feel *wanted*," murmured Esther, her big eyes round and thoughtful, her chin trembling with emotion.

"It might at that," agreed Angela, surprised again at the girl's insight. "Why don't you have a try?"

Later, undressing for bed in the room she and her mother were sharing for the week end, Angela repeated the conversation in a whisper. "That's not at all a bad idea," her mother said. "You know, Angie, I think you underrate Esther. She's a country girl, and a bit slow-moving, but she has a good heart. And she's not so stupid as you think."

"Boys-boys-boys," muttered Angela.

"That was last year," Mrs. Dodge chuckled, "when she was your age! This winter Esther is seventeen. She's growing up and getting some sense."

I'd rather be sixteen than seventeen any day, Angela thought; but she didn't say so, because immediately after the idea crossed her mind she wondered why.

Why—when she still had this *thing* about skiing?

Why—when she hadn't heard from Gregg?

And yet, there was the possibility that she might! As she lay in bed looking out of the open window at the distant stars, she wondered who had said, "Hope springs eternal in the human breast"? Of course there was also a Bible quotation: "Hope deferred maketh the heart sick." But her heart didn't feel sick; it felt fluttery and excited. Somehow, she thought, as she turned over and snuggled down into the blankets, I have a feeling I'll hear from Gregg soon.

A letter arrived, not soon, but just before Thanksgiving, and it was relatively unimportant. Gregg expected to be in Peru for a couple of days during Christmas vacation and he hoped they could ski together. Was she entering any of the standard races and, if so, how was she doing? "Some day," he promised in the last paragraph, "I'm going to teach you to jump!"

Angela waited a decent interval and then wrote back, trying to keep the same casual tone, anxious to conceal the fact that a single letter from Dartmouth could mean so much.

But her mother knew! "Angie," she said one day when they were alone, "remember you're only a junior in high school, dear. And Gregg is a college man. Don't be dismayed if he seeks the company of girls from Bennington or some other school. You are a little young for him."

"Sixteen—young?"

Janet smiled. "I think so."

"Gregg's only *just* nineteen," Angela remarked, but she began to give special attention to the Bennington girls who came to Bromley week ends,

to ski. They did look older—more sophisticated,
somehow. She wondered if Gregg would like her
better if she were more their type.

Then, realistically, she put the question out of her
mind. She was herself—Angela Dodge—and there
was no use pretending to be something she was not.
Gregg would like her or not on her own merits.
She'd bet he wasn't the only Dartmouth sophomore
who was friendly with a high-school girl!

There came a Saturday morning in mid-Decem-
ber when another letter arrived from Hanover. "Be
ready to ski with me!" Gregg wrote. "I'll be in
Peru the day after Christmas. Save me some time."

Just three sentences, but they were enough to
send Angela to Bromley on wings. She didn't look
around for Dave or any of the school crowd but
rode the lifts to the top, where she slipped off the
J-bar and skated over to the Corkscrew, which she
had not skied since last winter. For a few moments,
through a stroke of fate, she was completely alone.

It was a wonderful feeling! Angela looked down
on a world of brilliant winter white, where the only
discernible motion was made by the softly moving
clouds of her own breath. Far off she could see the
blue-green ranges of the mountains descending
into whitecaps and waves of hills which seemed to
break against the foot of the mountain on which
she stood. Below her were steeply ranked tiers of
evergreens and birches, some wearing cocked hats

of frost feathers. Between the trees lay the narrow, sharply falling gash of the trail, bordered by the deceptively soft-looking mounds made by snow-covered boulders. Far, far in the distance, a single skier, pin-point small, swooped momentarily into view.

Angela took a deep breath and glanced at her bindings, then pulled her goggles down over her eyes. She double-kicked to loosen the snow from the top of her skis and took a firm grip on her poles. Then she smiled, happily, joyfully, ready and anxious to take off. This, she thought, I will remember. This is a single great moment out of time.

She came down the upper Corkscrew like a dancer, as though she were interpreting some complicated movement in a ballet. Then she cut over to the Blue Ribbon and skied its length effortlessly, with the dash and daring of an expert. When she reached the bottom she was laughing with pure exhilaration, and she stopped with a quick jump turn, only to find herself gathered into Jacques Brunner's enfolding arms.

His heavy hands patted her back roughly. "You've got it!" he cried. "I watched you. You've got it!"

"I've got what?" Angie asked breathlessly.

"The fun. You're skiing for the fun of it again. It was beautiful—beautiful! Everything is now going to be all right."

The private pupil he had been instructing, a middle-aged man with a weather-tanned face, stood by and grinned. "If I could ski like that," he said, "I'd give five thousand bucks. Does it feel as good as it looks?"

Angie laughed. "Better!" she assured him. "It's wonderful. Better than anything else in the world!"

For the next two weeks, because it pleased Jacques and helped to take his mind off his great disappointment, Angela worked with renewed zest. She went into the weekly standard races and placed third and then second, which indicated her increasing skill in time measurement.

For Christmas, with extra money her mother had acquired by selling off some lumbering rights, Angela found under the Christmas tree a present which completely surprised her—new skis. They weren't fresh from a shop and unused (Jacques had made a good buy from one of his pupils), but— wonder of wonders!—they were Heads.

When she stroked them, with tears of delight and astonishment in her eyes, Jacques saved the situation by teasing her. "With these cheaters you can do anything. Wait and see!"

Angela "saw" that same afternoon. Compared to her old skis the new ones were like wings on her feet. They gave her a sense of effortless ease and complete confidence, and she could scarcely wait for Gregg to see how they handled, the next day.

With Gregg's arrival, of course, came an onrush
of other skiers, crowding the sissy slopes like the
Lord's Prayer and the Boulevard, and forcing Angie
and her mother and Chip all to bed down in the
same room. But after two years the guesthouse
routines were well established, and Chip was now
old enough to help Angela serve.

There was the inevitable houseful of adults and
their children, hearty, noisy, full of high spirits, all
set to spend the six days between Christmas and
New Year's Day on the mountain. As soon as they
clumped out of the place in the morning, Angie
cleaned up and hurried after, fully as avid as any
in the lot.

There came, wonder of wonders, two perfect
days. Each night it snowed, laying a fine powder
on the packed slopes. Together Angela and Gregg
skied all the expert trails, the Cork, the Blue, the
Peril—abbreviated to skiers' parlance—as well as the
Avalanche.

A year had given Gregg's style a certain finish.
"You're still so much better than I am!" Angela
panted in dismay as she caught up with him at the
bottom of a steep incline.

"Does that annoy you?" Gregg tried to conceal a
grin, but his eyebrows twitched impishly.

"It makes me want to improve."

"That's good," he said. "But remember this. A

man doesn't necessarily like a girl who can beat him at his own game."

Angela cocked her head thoughtfully. "I don't know quite what you mean."

"I mean I won't care a hoot if you don't ski better than you do right this minute. It simply isn't important, don't you see?"

Angela nodded, but actually she felt a little nonplused. Here was a masculine philosophy which she hadn't taken into consideration. In a way she understood; but still it was upsetting, because it undermined her competitive instinct. She still wanted to be better—to be best!

However, she had wonderful fun skiing with Gregg. When, on the second afternoon, he drove her back to the house in his uncle's car and said, "I wish this could go on for the whole week; I wish I didn't have to leave," she answered, "I wish you didn't either. It's been—it's been great!"

Gregg switched off the ignition and turned slightly in the seat. "Angie?"

"Yes?"

"I've been thinking about this, and wondering. You're a little young, but do you suppose your mother would let you come up for the Winter Carnival? We could ski on Moose Mountain. There'll be an outdoor pageant and dances and things. Besides, you'd see some of the best jumpers in the world!"

"Would I see you jump?"

"Maybe. I hope so."

Angela clasped her mittened hands and looked starry-eyed, but there was a good deal of uncertainty in her reply. "I'd love it," she said slowly, "but you know Mother counts on me, every week end there's snow. I'm not sure . . ."

"Let me talk to her," Gregg suggested.

But Angela shook her head. "It's my problem. Can I write you next week or do you have to know right now?"

Gregg smiled. "I can wait," he said. Then he reached over and covered her hands with one of his. "You're a funny girl," he said. "You're so direct. But it's comfortable, in a way, because a guy always knows where he stands."

CHAPTER *five*

ANGELA'S MOTHER SAID, "Yes, you may go," without equivocation. "It will be a marvelous experience for you—too good to miss."

"But how will you manage if the house is crowded with people that week end?"

"I'll get Esther to work full time."

Chip listened, big-eyed, to the plans. He was a little jealous of his sister and couldn't quite understand why she should have been invited. "I wish," he said enviously, "it was me."

Mrs. Dodge laughed and hugged him lightly. "I've never yet heard of an eleven-year-old boy being invited to the Dartmouth Winter Carnival," she told him. Then she turned back to Angela. "You'll need a new party dress."

Inured, by now, to a stringent economy, it seemed fantastic to Angie to be talking in these terms. A party dress. Bus fare. Spending money. "Can we afford it, Mother?" she asked anxiously.

"We will afford it," Mrs. Dodge replied with determination. "This is important. Besides, we're solvent this year, for a change."

Indeed, the family outlook was considerably brighter. The bunkhouse was rapidly paying for itself, snow had come early, and the Dodges' hospitality was now a byword among skiers from far and near.

Angela lived through the next weeks in a walking dream, even though she managed to pass her midyears competently. Nothing seemed real, not even the bus ride to Hanover. The winter landscape flew by like a motion picture and she didn't have time to wonder whether Gregg would be ashamed of her, because she hadn't "been around" much or because she might not have brought quite the right clothes.

The town itself seemed like something out of a storybook. Settled snugly in its broad valley, it was jammed with thousands of carnivalites, press men, radio announcers, photographers, movie makers, and just plain visitors. The crunch of their feet on the snow made a kind of music, and the elaborate snow and ice sculptures in front of the fraternity houses and dormitories were dwarfed only by the huge center-of-campus statue of an Indian incongruously holding an alpenhorn.

Toting Angela's skis over his shoulder and her suitcase in his free hand, Gregg led her happily to the room which she was to share with three other girls for the week end. "We're in luck!" he said. "The snow conditions are dandy. Get into your ski things and I'll give you a look at the Vale of Tempe."

It took only ten minutes to change, and once Angie was in pants and parka, all sense of uneasiness fled. Tomorrow night at the Carnival Ball she might feel like a fish out of water, but in these clothes she was happy and at home.

Crossing the campus, Gregg pointed out the college landmarks proudly—the white Georgian serenity of Dartmouth Row, the tower of Baker Library, which was so much like Independence Hall, the giant elms flanking the Common.

But it was the ski jump, famous from coast to coast, which impressed Angela most. Carefully manicured for the big week end, it looked lightning-fast. "Goodness," she said, watching a jumper who was practicing, "you mean you can take off through the air like that and land right side up?"

"Most of the time. Not always. Wait and see me —and wish me luck."

Today they were allowed to ski anywhere except on the slalom and downhill courses, which were ready and waiting for the intercollegiate events. It was fun to be on new trails, fun to have Gregg guide her and wait for her if she fell behind. Angela's cheeks became wind-painted and her eyes bright. "Oh, Gregg!" she cried spontaneously, "I've never had such a good time."

"This is just the beginning," he promised, and proved to be right.

The big extravaganza in the Snow Bowl, where an outdoor evening had been planned, made Angela feel as though she were discovering fairyland. Pair by pair, the undergraduates and their dates filed under a huge snow arch, while yellow torchlight flickered on expectant faces, and every now and then a girl was plucked from her escort to be whisked away by some Outing Club scout and considered with a few other lucky visitors for the title of Carnival Queen.

It amused Angela to watch the process, and to note the aggrieved expressions on the faces of the lads who lost their girls. "You can't blame them," Gregg said when she commented on it. "Once a girl is chosen Queen, you might as well kiss her good-by. As a matter of fact, to be quite accurate, you're lucky if you get the chance! You've spent good money on her, and what have you got on your hands? A celebrity. That's all."

"But doesn't it give a man a kind of prestige?"

"Prestige—what's that?" Gregg snorted. "It doesn't get you back your girl."

They grew silent then, as the program started.

Searchlights cut through the darkness, following
the balletlike movements of a famous figure skater
on the rink below. From a loud-speaker came lilt-
ing dance music, interspersed with announcements
and introductions. Then came a skiing exhibition,
featuring an acrobatic junior who did a forward
somersault off a jump, landed in precarious balance,
and flashed down a slope into the arena, to a burst
of enthusiastic applause.

One event followed another and finally, after a
dramatic blackout, the Queen was crowned while
rockets flared in the sky. She was a tall, slender,
blue-eyed blonde from Smith College, who looked
both pleased and slightly dazed, even though she
kept smiling gamely. After what Gregg had said,
Angela didn't envy her. "I'm glad I'm not pretty,"
she whispered. "I'd rather be with you."

Gregg chuckled and tucked Angie's hand through
his arm. "You are pretty," he told her, "in an out-
door-y kind of way. And tomorrow you'll have to
get set to spend most of the day without me, because I'll be skiing in the jumping competition and
the slalom."

It was very cold the next morning—fourteen
degrees below zero—but Angela slipped out of bed
early, anxious not to miss any of the events. This
was the best skiing she was likely to see in many
a day, and the prospect thrilled her. She pulled on
her long red underwear and ski pants hastily but

quietly, careful not to awaken any of her three roommates, who were still curled deep under the covers and likely to remain there for a couple of hours to come.

But she was in for a surprise. A dark head was thrust up like a turtle's, and a girl whom she remembered only as Betty asked in a whisper, "Is your date a skier?"

Angela nodded.

"Wait a sec!" Betty commanded as she threw back the covers. "I'm coming too."

Together, carrying their ski boots in their hands, the two girls crept down to the front hall, where several other hardy souls were already gathered around a coffee urn. They laced up their boots and joined them, feeling the hot liquid warm and stimulate them, then breakfasted hungrily, astonished that so many other girls were already up and out.

Betty, Angela discovered, went to Colby College, and her date was racing in the downhill but not in the slalom. He proved to be a string bean of a lad with a devil-may-care attitude. When he plummeted down the icy, bumpy trail, risking all he dared, and stopped the clock for a well-deserved fourth against the nation's top collegians, Betty grabbed Angela's arm in excitement and jumped up and down for joy.

As the morning advanced, the crowd thickened, everyone stamping cold feet, clapping their hands to stimulate circulation, and keeping their eyes turned toward the slalom course, which was dotted with an intricate pattern of red and blue flags. "The hill looks as though it's in good shape," Angela commented, to make conversation, but inside she felt as apprehensive as though she herself were among the huddle of skiers waiting at the top.

A man's voice came over the loud-speaker, announcing the race, and the lads began to peel off, one by one, as Angie hugged herself and waited for Gregg's name to be called.

Meanwhile, she watched half a dozen visiting collegians speed down the tricky course. Their knowledge of slopes and fall lines, their grasp of flag combinations, was apparent even at this distance. Here was competition at its keenest. As Gregg had promised, it was a thrilling spectacle to watch.

"Number 37. Harrison of Dartmouth."

Angela caught her breath, and watched the minuscule figure far up on the slope stretch out for his lunge. "Go, go, go!" she breathed, unconscious that she was talking out loud. "Get in there, Gregg! Faster!"

She could see him blast the top in-line gates with no visible checking. He took a flush as though it were child's play, spurted through some S-gates off to the left, then traversed the fall line at high speed, coming toward a hairpin turn on the right.

"Watch that booby trap!" Angela yelled as he approached another hairpin by traversing a steep pitch. Two of the previous racers had come a cropper there.

Betty glanced toward her companion with a grin. "He can't hear you," she reminded Angie.

But Angela was beyond caring. She wasn't standing here near the finish line with a thousand or more spectators. She was up there on the mountain, racing against time. Every turn, every schuss, she felt in her bones. Even her breath came short, until Gregg came into the straightaway and flashed across the finish line, with more authority than she had ever seen him display.

Admiring comments broke out all around the two girls, because the crowd felt that it had glimpsed greatness. "He's only a sophomore, I understand. By next year—!"

"By next year," somebody predicted, "he'll be tops!"

When the times were all in, Gregg placed third, an enviable spot, a credit to Dartmouth. Yet he didn't seem unduly elated when he joined Angela and took her back to the village for lunch. "It was a good race," he said. "The snow conditions were swell, except for one sneaky little passage. Did you see me almost come to grief?"

"I thought you skied magnificently," Angela said, and meant it.

They ate steaming bowls of soup and cheese-burgers and chocolate layer cake, while Angela's toes thawed out and the tip of her nose lost its bright pink hue. "I never realized how cold you could get standing still," she admitted. "But I loved every minute of it."

The big show, however, was to be the jumping, and for this the morning crowd was tripled. Gregg told Angie exactly where to place herself for the best view, and hurried off with only one backward glance and a descriptive circle formed by thumb and index finger. "Wish me luck!" it said.

"Oh, I do, I do!" Angela murmured, although he was already out of earshot.

Betty had rejoined her date, so this afternoon Angie was alone, but she didn't mind. This was a spectacle such as she had never before witnessed, and because she had never jumped, she could no longer identify herself with Gregg. She knew he was up there with the team members at the top, but he might as well have been a stranger about to come out for a vaudeville act.

Stationed on a knoll which commanded a clear view of the course, she listened to the announcer. "Three leaps, the best two out of three to count in the scoring."

She watched the first man on the Dartmouth team crouch for the take-off and soar through the

air with the calmness of an eagle, to land at the
125-foot marker. "Beautiful!" she breathed.

But at the same time she knew that it was more
than beauty she was watching. It was agility and
grace, combined with lightning reactions and courage. This was more than skiing; it was snowman-
ship.

A Middlebury jumper made a faultless landing,
to the applause of the crowd. Then another Dartmouth team member swam through the air, to spill
in the transition. End over end he tumbled, stunned
and rattled, but he gathered himself together
quickly and trudged back up the hill.

Gregg's name was announced, and Angela leaned
forward tensely. She saw him throw his body
forward and upward at the take-off, following
through the swing of the arms. Flying, he seemed
to lean forward from the ankles with a slight bend
from the hips, so that the upper part of his body
was approximately parallel to his skis. Downward
he soared, seeking a landing place, and just before
the moment of impact she gasped. Would he make
it?

He would! In a springy Telemark position he
came from the transition into the flat of the outrun.
"That's the lad who came in third in the slalom,"
someone said. "He's sure got style."

Angela agreed, but realized that the distance he

made wasn't exceptional. His second run bettered
the first by only a foot, but on his third leap, giving
it all he had, he seemed to approach the take-off as
a dive bomber approaches a target.

"Now!" Angie cried, and felt everything Gregg
had go into the lift. For a long moment he seemed
to hang motionless, a superman painted against the
blue of the sky. Then he dropped—slowly, slowly—
to a feather-soft landing, and as he christied to a
stop on the outrun the applause was quick and
sincere.

They liked him. He still wasn't up with the top
distance men, but he was stylish. He looked good.
He had a certain flare.

At the Carnival Ball that evening Angela had her
first taste of living in reflected glory. A dozen or
more of Gregg's classmates came over to congratulate him, and he grinned and thanked them shyly.
"Next to the big boys I'm still a neophyte," he
said.

"Neophyte nothing. You're a comer," a teammate
insisted. "All you have to do is get a little more
experience. We've got a lot of skiing to do yet
before we leave this school!"

"I'll say we have!"

"Two more years," counted Angela as they
danced away.

Gregg looked down at her almost tenderly.

"Where are you going to college? Have you thought?"

"Middlebury, maybe, if I can get a scholarship and earn some money on the side."

Nodding approvingly, Gregg said, "Fine. When I'm an old harassed businessman I can come over and watch you go through your paces."

"What paces?"

"My pet," Gregg said, "I've been trying to tell you since the first day you fell at my feet that your skiing potential is terrific. If I were a betting man I'd hazard ten bucks that in three years you'll make me look as if I were standing still."

Angela laughed at the mere idea. "Never!"

"I won't argue," Gregg countered. "Just wait and see."

Giving herself up to the rhythm of the music, Angela didn't speak for a minute or two. Then she said, frankly thoughtful, "I'm not sure which I'd like better, being a very good skier myself or being proud of you."

Gregg pulled her to him affectionately. "That is a very sweet—and a very feminine—thing to have said."

Later, walking home in the still, soft whiteness, with snow falling gently from the midnight sky, they heard the clock on Baker begin to toll the hour, and Angela listened to each deep-throated chime echoing through the hills.

"It has been the most wonderful week end," she said softly. "Everything. Wonderful!"

"For me, too," Gregg murmured, squeezing her hand.

ANGELA AND HER MOTHER stood with their arms around each other's shoulders, looking out of the kitchen window and giggling uncontrollably, like a couple of schoolgirls. In the back pasture, flushed to a bright crimson and looking larger than life, was Esther Byley—on skis!

Jacques was teaching her to snowplow, and Esther was working with fierce concentration, her normally smooth brow furrowed by parallel ridges of anxiety, her full mouth set in a determined, tight-lipped line.

"Good!" They could hear Jacques call. "Splendid!"

"How can he say that?" Angela exclaimed. "She's on her fanny more often than on her feet."

"At least she's trying," Mrs. Dodge said, when she could stop laughing. "As far as I can discover, Marie didn't even do that."

Angela's eyes widened. "You mean—?"

Her mother nodded, sobering for a moment. "I think we have a budding romance."

"With Esther? Why, she's only a year older than I am."

"I know, but I think she's the type to marry young and raise a big family. Some of these country girls mature early, you know."

Esther took another spill, sprawling headlong this time. As she picked herself up and dusted the snow off her front industriously, Jacques again demonstrated the spread necessary in the snowplow technique.

"But—but do you think Jacques is actually falling in love with her?" Angela asked doubtfully.

"It's too early to tell, but at least he isn't moping around the house any more," said her mother. "And Esther is positively transfigured. Haven't you noticed? She sings at her work."

"Who sings at her work?" Chip asked, coming into the room with a dog comb and brush. Without waiting for an answer, he asked, "Where's Christie? I've got to groom him. Mr. Nickerson says I must do it every day now before the show."

"What show?" asked Angela.

"The dog show at Bennington next Saturday. We've got both of our setters entered, Mr. Nickerson and me."

"And I," corrected Mrs. Dodge automatically. "Call him, Chip. I think he's outside."

When the big bronze dog galloped into the room, Angela looked at him appraisingly. "He's a sweetie-pie," she said, " a real darling, but do you actually think he's got any of the points of a show dog, Chip?"

Her brother glared at her reproachfully. "Look at that muzzle!" he cried. "Feel the gloss of that coat!" He arranged Christie in show stance, a hand under his chin. "I bet he gets a blue ribbon—or at least a red or yellow." Then suddenly he leaned forward and put both arms around Christie's neck, giving him an ardent bear hug. "And even if he loses I'll still love him," he announced cheerfully. "He's the most wonderful dog in the whole world!"

Angela remembered this remark a fortnight later, as she stood at the top of the course laid out for the Holiday Cup Race. Somewhere near the finish line Gregg would be waiting. "And even if I come in last, he'll still . . . well, *like* me," she said to herself, and smiled.

It was a sparkling day, but the snow was old, and the course was fast and tricky. Jacques had groomed her for this race, her first try at an open event, and he had confidence in her, but Angela knew that she would be competing against skiers far more experienced than herself.

Still, she felt full of happy anticipation. The butterflies which made her stomach queasy were no more than normal. "Every racer gets them," Gregg had told her. "If he doesn't he isn't worth his salt."

Because she wanted Jacques to be proud of her, because her mother and Chip were watching, but most of all because Gregg was here for the week end, Angela wanted to do well. She knew that she was prepared to give her utmost, but she also knew that she could be a good loser, if necessary. Never again would the urge to win be so overpowering that it shattered her control.

At the same time she was filled with a new spirit, learned from watching Gregg and the rest of the skiers at Dartmouth. She felt daring, ready to extend herself, ready to reach a little farther than ever before. And she had one great advantage over all the visitors. She knew the course like the back of her hand!

The first of the racers was moving forward into the slot. Angela saw her grab a lungful of air and get set for the "go" signal, watched her drive forward with her poles. She was off, swooping down the hemlock-stitched trail like a rocket, out of sight now as Angela adjusted her racing bib and moved forward in line.

"A deep crouch on a steep slope can increase your

top speed by as much as a third," Jacques had reminded her at breakfast. She must remember that.
Her mind seemed to be racing ahead of her body;
it was filled with a thousand thoughts and memories
which glinted like the sunlight on the snow. She
felt alive—alive and alert as never before, and the
air was like wine in her veins.

Another racer started, then another. Angela was
next. Now! she said to herself. Now.

"Four . . . three . . . two . . . one. . . ." The starter
tapped her on the back. "Go!"

Swooping down over the glistening course, bare-
headed, in the spectacular, driving style which
Jacques had taught her, Angela's low-flying figure
stretched toward the tips of her skis. The snow,
violet-blue in the shadow of the firs, was dazzling
in the sunlight. She squinted against the glare, dis-
daining goggles, and grinned in pure delight.

Crouch! Lower to avoid wind resistance. Up a
little for a necessary check. With parallel turns she
made every second count, and when she dared she
schussed, taking the moguls straight on limber legs.

The crowd at the base of the trail were a blur as
she plunged down a precipitous incline. Snow-
clouded, she christied and swept down another
dizzying descent, with the verve and courage
inherited from her father.

The fastest line! Always the fastest line. Yet a

watch-tick moment of bad judgment, a split second out of control, and she knew she could go careening off the downhill course at a fatal sixty-mile-an-hour clip.

Like every other racer, she talked to herself out loud. "Faster now. Faster! Go, go, go!" Speed and control. Speed and control. The finish line was rushing toward her. Oh, what fun! she thought. What wonderful fun!

It was a good run, she knew, but she didn't guess how good until times were announced. Gretchen Harvey, a top skier and frequent winner from Stowe, took the cup, but Angela's time was just one second behind.

Suddenly she found herself surrounded. Jacques was clapping her on the back, Gregg was shouting congratulations, her mother was standing by in happy astonishment, and Chip was looking at her as though she were a stranger, he was so impressed.

Only Dave Colby, who joined the group belatedly and stood rocking back and forth with his hands in the pockets of his ski pants, failed to look surprised. "I told you so," he said, as though it were all his doing. "I told you she was an angel on skis."

Everybody laughed, because it was so apparent that Dave considered Angie his find, his pupil. All the weeks and months she had spent training with Jacques he discounted. "You ought to see what she can do in jodhpur boots with a pair of broomstick poles," he bragged.

"With snow rings made from Crisco cans," put in Chip.

Angela was not embarrassed. "Do you still think you could get me a spot on television, Dave?"

"You'll be on television some day," Jacques promised seriously, "when you're trying out for the Olympics. You've got what it takes."

Angela shook her head. "I'm still second-best," she reminded him.

"If I could have been second-best at sixteen, Angie," Jacques remarked quietly, "there's no place I couldn't have gone."

Gregg kept nodding his head. "That's right. You tell her. Some day she's going to be great!"

"Great?" Angela murmured. "I doubt it." It was a word which didn't mean much to her, actually. "I've learned one thing, though, thanks to Jacques," she felt impelled to say. "I can't ski well unless I'm having fun."

To celebrate, everybody lunched at the Boar's Head, carrying their trays to a table in a far corner, and toasting Angela with their coffee.

"To the skier I discovered!" quipped Dave.

"To my most promising pupil!" Jacques said, with a ceremonious bow.

But it was Gregg who capped the climax and

offered the most memorable pledge of all. With his shaggy eyebrows tilted rakishly and his face alight with pride and pleasure, he raised his coffee cup as though it were a champagne glass and said, very clearly, "To my best girl!"